WALDO

Paul Theroux

WALDO

a novel by

Paul Theroux

Houghton Mifflin Company Boston

1967

First Printing   c

For Craig Wylie and John Lindberg

". . . Baader, who calls himself President of the World, is the father of three children. He has twice been locked up by mistake in a lunatic asylum. He is not an especially interesting man, but certainly a very genial one. On the occasion of the death of his wife, he delivered a long oration to the three thousand people at the funeral, contending that death is essentially a Dadaist affair. He was wearing a smile on his lips. He had, none the less, been very fond of his wife . . ."

TRISTAN TZARA
Memoirs of Dadaism

Part One

Chapter One

Who would have guessed that Waldo would later hobnob with grown women in hotel rooms for weeks on end, be hailed as a blazing new talent of the semi-surrealistic non-fiction novel and be solely responsible for making one of his neighbors a Mother of the Year?

No one in his right mind would associate that man of talent ("full of wit and verve" as one critic described him) with the delinquent boy now standing in the Mess Hall of the Booneville School for Delinquent Boys and watching the cream pie sailing through the air.

Waldo knew it would hurt. It was tilted forward and spun sweet gobs in a spiral as it came at him. The pie hit Waldo in the face with a big blind smash. The pie broke and the juice ran down his neck.

"My mother's got more guts than all your old ladies put together," one boy had said.

Waldo, a bit hesitantly because he was not brave, asked the boy if by any chance that meant his mother was a very fat woman, a big cow maybe?

Then he got hit with the pie. The pie plate bruised his nose and as he licked the cream from his cheeks he was punched. He fell, was perhaps kicked, and with a smile went out cold.

Lying on the cool floor Waldo's entire being withdrew without a murmur to his head. His mind traveled back over four months. There he was asking the U.S. Marshal with the big hat for permission to go up to the first car of the train, since it would be his last train ride for some time.

"Just get yer ass back here toot sweet," said the Marshal. He was an old hand at taking boys to prison. He knew they were too scared to jump from a moving train. Years ago they would have jumped, but nowadays they just didn't have the gumption.

Standing in a draft at the front of the first car of the train Waldo could make out the head and neck of the engineer in the cab sweating in the light of a bare bulb. Above the engineer's cap, outside, Waldo had seen the silhouette of the smokestack — like a cannon aimed against the delicate threads of the trees. The smokestack glowed in the moonlight along with the other pipes and knobs of the locomotive. The train chugged and clattered across the silence of the woods.

The moon dripped its meringue on the trees and the engineer reached up and yanked on a chain. A volley of steam exploded from the whistle, clouding the moon and obscuring the trees. Things went dark. It was night. A snake of steam and smoke flopped alongside the train as the train rushed on. This smoke made the bars on the outside become visible; and still the blue arm of the engineer yanked against the inky darkness and shot out the steam and smoke and made the window-bars visible in front of Waldo's face.

Waldo looked hard out the window of the train. The smoke cleared and the moon smacked its lips and reassured Waldo. The moon was firm, and soon the moon was Warden Deed. Waldo was being jogged along on a stretcher.

Because the Booneville School for Delinquent Boys was a model prison it looked like a supermarket. It was a sprawling house of glass where boys were brought to their senses and rehabilitated. The day of the whip was gone. It went with the torture chamber and the roach-strewn cells. The guiding motto of Booneville was: Boys Will Be Boys. Where there were once thick iron bars now were lovely large shatterproof panes of glass, and inside the glass with earnest young faces were once-delinquent boys looking out.

"Through broken homes and bad breaks and bent marriages," said Warden Deed using his own geometry, "these boys have not been given a square deal. This bum luck starts to harden them up. Booneville shapes them up good and proper, makes them good, grateful citizens and real patriots, teaches them a trade and most of all helps them out."

In a magazine article in the *Saturday Evening Post* entitled, "Warden Deed Wants You — To Listen!" he was quoted as saying, "The only thing Booneville can't offer is a chance to see the world. That's just got to come later."

"At this point in time you've got to remember you're not dealing with crooks. They're not jailbirds," said the Warden, "they're boys."

Waldo was injured. His face hurt from the pie plate and his ribs ached from the kick. He was put into the prison hospital to mend. The doctor came to see him and told him he wanted to help him, that he wanted to straighten him out. This doctor — his name was Wasserman — told Waldo that he had an aggression problem. He advised Waldo to learn a trade.

Cooking was underrated as a profession, he said. The best cooks were men. A good short order cook could always find work. People were crying for them. Wasserman added that cooks made a lot of (ha-ha) dough and if you were a cook you would never go hungry.

Waldo said he would think it over. He looked out the window of the hospital wing to the kitchen wing. There was some grass and flowers in between the wings. The kitchen wing was made entirely of glass: a glass aquarium where the cooking was done and a glass corridor which ran around the aquarium. There was a good reason for this. The boys were not to be reminded that they were being punished, that they were "inside," captive. The glass walls were to give the impression that the boys were on a long picnic in the country. The glass was kept very clean and it was nearly invisible. It was shatterproof, bulletproof and hard as steel. The kitchen was the glassiest of all the wings. It was a rectangle of chrome and stoves entirely encased in seamless panes of glass.

Waldo wondered whether he should try cooking. He told Wasserman that he was not so much interested in work as in money itself. Waldo knew that the kitchen provided a good view of the Booneville Valley, the trees, the fat sun. Going to cooking class would be a lot like going to the movies. It would be fun, the safest kind of fun, watching. But Waldo did not finally decide to be a cook until he heard that there were real goings-on in the Booneville Kitchen. The boys had learned to make Booneville Gin.

After four classes Waldo approached a Negro with bristling hair and a blotched face. Waldo had expected the boy to be black, but the boy was not black. He was brown and looked bruised. Waldo had heard a rumor that the boy had been elected Attorney General of a southern state; another rumor said that the boy was a rapist, a cop-killer and a dope fiend; and still another claimed that he had carried signs and barged into lunch counters. Waldo happened to know that the Negro's name was Otto Noon.

"Real gin?" Waldo asked.

"Yeah," said Noon, "we make it out of sugar and malt and crap."

A guard came over. "Lessee them molds," he said.

They were supposed to be on fudge bars. Otto Noon produced his pan filled with neat troughs of fudge dough.

"Cook 'em up and then shoot 'em down to the wrappers,"

said the guard. "We gotta get out twenny-two duz today."
The guard turned to Waldo. "You unnerstan' what ya supposed to do?"

"I guess so," said Waldo.

"Don't guess," said the guard, "you'll get into trouble that
way."

"I'm in trouble now, aren't I?"

"You could do worse," said the guard. "I seen guys do
worse. Noon here'll tell you all about it." He dunked his
finger into the liquid fudge dough, then licked it. "Help
Noon. I'll be over the wrapping table — so no screwing
around." He was gone.

As Otto Noon slid the pan into the oven and set the ther-
mostat at the correct temperature he said, "This here is what
Booneville is famous for — fudge bars."

"No kidding," said Waldo with not much enthusiasm.

"No shit," said Noon. Then he said impatiently, "So you
wanna swill some or not? I ain't got all day."

"If there's any around."

"I told you we got some homemade Booneville Gin. You
think I'm bird-turding?"

"Okay," said Waldo.

"Wait'll the screw leaves or we'll get fuzzed. If they catch
us our ass'll be in a crack."

Waldo was silent. He looked over at the guard. The guard
was eating and talking. Otto Noon busily clanged pans when
he saw the guard eyeing him.

"When the screw leaves we hit the gin," said Noon.

"Isn't he supposed to be guarding us?"

"This is Booneville, man. Boys are boys. He'll leave, and
when he does he'll put dumb-ass over there in charge. He's
so unfudgingconscious he won't know what's going on."

Waldo looked at the boy called dumb-ass. He was on fudge
bars, too.

"I been cheesed-off at him for weeks," said Noon casting a mean glance at dumb-ass. And then Noon looked at Waldo and said, "You in or out?"

"In."

"It costs."

"How much?"

"Pack of weeds."

The guard stood at the wrapping table craning his neck and munching a fudge bar. After a while he beckoned to the boy called dumb-ass, said something to him, slapped him on the back and left by slipping past the rear oven. He had trouble with the sliding door, a large piece of nearly invisible glass with a tiny groove for a handle. He moved the door open a crack and ducked out.

Otto Noon walked quietly over to dumb-ass. He spoke softly and as he did a giant of a boy stepped behind him. This boy, oily-skinned and sneaky, was Erratio Lizardi. He was wearing a mushroom-type chef's hat and there was a large banana of flesh on the back of his neck. He placed his hands on his hips, gulped down his smile in one swallow and looked at dumb-ass and said one word.

"Fungoo."

He did not even attempt an Italian accent.

Otto Noon jerked his thumb over his shoulder. Dumb-ass looked at Lizardi and dug his toe into the floor nervously. It was decided that dumb-ass should have the first drink. Lizardi got a glass of gin and gave it to him.

"If he spills a drop I'll ram this here ladle up his bucket." Noon waved the ladle at dumb-ass.

Dumb-ass swallowed the whole glass of gin. Nausea passed through his body like a large descending lump, causing him to bump forward and wag his head. Tears came to his eyes.

"He likes it," said Lizardi.

"Now *you're* in this," said Noon, jabbing the ladle at dumb-ass. "So don't sing or you'll get fuzzed too. And watch out because I been cheesed-off at you for weeks."

"I been cheesed-off at him too," said Lizardi. "That's all I been for weeks."

The boys formed two lines. Noon took charge of one line, Lizardi the other. Both ladled out the gin into the empty fudge molds which the boys brought up. One by one the boys returned to the tables to guzzle their gin. And soon the whole rectangle of glass resembled the model kitchen that it was. The boys stood in neat clusters at the work tables, each boy with a fudge mold brimming with homemade Booneville Gin. Once, while they were all quietly assembled at the tables, Warden Deed pressed his nose against the glass and looked in. The boys looked up and smiled at the Warden and then returned to their fudge molds.

"They're not thugs," Warden Deed mumbled to himself, and he walked away.

Noon faced Waldo. "You in or out?"

Waldo thought a moment. He looked at the boys drinking the stuff. It was certainly against the rules. *Rules?* And then Waldo looked at the panes of glass which sealed him in the kitchen and thought: *I'm in prison*. I'm already *in* prison. Where could they possibly put me for breaking the rules of the prison? If you didn't break rules, thought Waldo, then what are you doing in prison?

"In," said Waldo, and taking a large pan full of gin he thought: the President is probably a lush. He sucked at the gin and looked out past the glass edges, past the tile corridor, past the bulletproof, shatterproof, cold-sealed double pane of the outer wall to the long slope of the Booneville Valley. The valley was covered with patches of bushes, each leafless bush looking cold and barren, and the whole slope darkening red in the sun now setting behind the jagged tops of the trees. Like black teeth on a huge lower jaw, the trees seemed to be biting the red sun in half.

Waldo stood locked in his thoughts, but soon became aware of laughter, joyous laughter, beginning slowly from different parts of the aquarium. The boys could have been little fish, the laughter bubbles. Waldo turned and saw the boys staggering and singing; some leaped and kicked and threw their arms and legs in all directions; some danced and embraced each other and made no secret of their affection. Some retched.

The boy called dumb-ass was picking things up from the floor and giggling. He said he was tidying the place up. He saw a scrap of paper lying outside the glass, but when he went for it he was thrown back by the clean pane.

Waldo noticed that neither Noon nor Lizardi had drunk too much. They were rummaging through the drawers for things. They carried aerosol cans, cake decorators and frosting brushes to the center of the room. As the drunken boys limped about the room bleary-eyed Noon and Lizardi began dumping chocolate on them and spraying them with whipped cream. The boys, one by one, were turned into giant éclairs. As they fell Noon sprinkled them with chopped nuts.

"Stay loose!" Noon said, now riding Lizardi and walloping the drunks on the head with a saucepan. The drunks fought back with sticky fists. Otto Noon dug his heels into Lizardi and shouted, "Gee-dap!"

It was war. The drunks feebly threw things at Noon and his mount. Noon saw the angry boys, scooped up a hand mixer and used it to bore their frosted flesh. Then the wrestling started, Noon and the others rolling in the flour; meanwhile Lizardi amused himself by writing obscenities in sugary frosting on the boys that had passed out.

Waldo watched a boy take Noon and push him up against

the glass wall. He saw figures approaching from the other side of the wall. The guards.

The guards! The guards spread out around the glass. Waldo was worried; he wondered whether he should leave through the sliding door. But the guards were there, just standing in the glass corridor with their clubs.

Waldo was about five feet from an oven, one of those huge institutional ovens, greasy, sooty, glass-fronted. Waldo edged over to the oven slowly, put his fudge mold of gin on the floor, climbed into the oven, crouched down and pulled the door shut. On all fours Waldo peered through the oven window; caged like a cooking goose.

Noon saw the guards and shouted to Lizardi. Lizardi dropped his frosting-gun and rushed to the opposite wall, where the sun had been, didn't see the glass, and knocked himself to the floor, backward, as tiny threads of crack appeared in a web where his head had hit the glass.

Noon was four inches from a laughing guard and he swung his fist at the guard's jaw, shielded now by the glass. Noon punched the glass, his wrist bent, he yelped and darted to another wall. When he tried to leap into a corridor he was caught mid-flight and thrown to the floor.

The whole kitchen was swarming with the white frosted forms of the dazed boys who bumped against the glass. Outside the glass the guards nudged each other and taunted the boys, clownish in the flour and running against the bullet-proof, shatterproof panes of glass, breaking themselves against it.

Waldo cowered in the stove safe from the panic in the kitchen, his face still pressed against the glass of the oven door. He could see the boys being smacked back into the center of the kitchen as they rebounded from the hard walls. One boy near the far wall found the nearly invisible groove in the sliding door. He got the door open and started to leave, but a guard dashed over and clubbed him on the head. Blood spurted over the white flour, congealing it into red lumps.

Through this door and over the body of the clubbed boy entered the guards; they milled and thrashed among the struggling flour-covered boys. The shouting of the guards bewildered the boys even more; they stopped leaping and running at the glass. The guards hammered down with their clubs, beating the boys into the invisible corners of the kitchen. Waldo realized that they were expending all their energy to hurt. They were grown men, not very strong, hitting only to hurt. Still Waldo watched.

Soon the kitchen was still, all the boys propped in bent postures, a cloud of flour in the air. The guards wiped the flour from their suits and tried to restore the gray. To Waldo the powder in the air and the gray-suited forms looked like a dream in which he was not involved. He tried to squirm into the back of the stove but in moving he dislodged the front of the oven which fell open with a loud slap. Waldo squatted in the oven, exposed.

The guards turned and looked at Waldo. Waldo trembled and tried to speak, but he found he could not shape the words. He felt as if he were screaming, but he could hear nothing. He thought of leaping from the oven. He started to edge forward when one red-faced guard puffed up to him and pushed his hand in Waldo's face, forcing him back into the oven. The guard was still gasping for breath as he clapped the oven door shut on Waldo.

The sounds stopped. Waldo put his eyeball against the glass and saw the bloodshot eyes of the prison guard not two inches away. Waldo yelled to him, but this time Waldo heard the yell trapped inside his little oven and he stopped. The guard shrugged.

Soon all the guards were around the oven, looking through

the glass and pushing each other away from the front. Eight fat faces fitted themselves on the glass and blocked the light. Waldo crouched in the darkness.

After several minutes some light filtered through and Waldo saw the guards clump to the side of the oven. They reached toward the top, their arms and faces melting together in the dreamlike effect which the rippled glass of the oven produced.

Waldo felt the heat almost immediately. The walls and the floor of the oven came instantly hot. Waldo squirmed, tried to flap his arms, but could not straighten them. Like a bird, blistering although fully-clothed and, worst of all, alive, Waldo squawked and ignored the awful sound it made in his ears. He stopped trying to flap his arms, stopped pleading and began banging his head against the top of the oven in an attempt to knock himself unconscious.

He did not have to bang long. The heat of the oven made his whole body ring with pain. He jerked up once, then whimpered and fell beak-first into the glass front of the oven. The last thing Waldo remembered was the sharp stench of his burning skin and hair.

Waldo looked up at, but not through, the rimless glasses of the Staff Nurse. He saw reflected on them a dome of bandages and some eyes and some thick white paws. He went back to sleep. When he awoke he saw a cigar. Beyond the cigar was Wasserman.

Wasserman said that Warden Deed would hush the whole thing up, even the death of the clubbed boy. Waldo would be better soon; his hair had to grow back, his burns had to heal. Wasserman said that he would get Waldo placed in the library.

"The question," said Warden Deed one month later, "is did you or didn't you take a drink?"

"Yes," said Waldo.

"Go on," said the Warden.

"Yes, I did take a drink."

"Splendid. Now I'm going to be more than fair. I'm going to give you five extra months to sober up. You can think of it as sort of a hangover."

As Waldo added five and nine Warden Deed told him to send the next boy in. There were two boys talking rapidly outside the Warden's office. When Waldo heard the name of Otto Noon he edged closer and listened.

"Bashed on the conk. That's what Pickles said."

"Pickles said that?"

"He'll prolly wig off. That's what happens to guys that get bashed. They wig off."

"He'll wig off," said the smaller boy. "If he got conked like you said."

"Someone said he was cheesed-off at dumb-ass cause dumb-ass called him a lousy spade. But dumb-ass didn't do it. A screw did."

"Too bad."

"Bad? A conked spade!" He faced the smaller boy and said thoughtfully, "A conked spade. That's worse than having the double clap!"

"The double clap? I never heard of no double clap. Is it like the regular clap?"

"Worse."

"You're next," said Waldo.

The riot was soon forgotten and the months went by very fast. Waldo was not sure whether he liked it or not. He was sure he was not making money — he didn't like that. And now he was sure he was in the pen. The riot had convinced everyone of that. Before the riot everyone had called Boone-ville "the home" or "the school." Now it was "the pen."

Warden Deed's faith in boys was shaken only slightly by

the riot. As Wasserman had predicted Warden Deed did hush everything up. Waldo waited for some signal from the outside, some sign that would prove that the riot had been written up in all the papers. But the weekly postcards from home bore no trace of knowing. They all began "Dear Son" and ended with the usual "always your Mom & Dad" under the usual "Keep Pluggin." Waldo wrote that he had to stay five more months and that was that.

Waldo visited Wasserman twice a week. Wasserman had gone to the dead boy's funeral and talked to the dead boy's mother who said that she couldn't believe it, thought that it would never happen in her family; other families maybe, but not hers. Still the dead boy, her son, looked so peaceful there, not a wrinkle on his face, like he was sleeping, and so on.

He wasn't a bad kid, Wasserman said. He had been trying at Booneville. Everyone at the funeral said what a nice kid he was, what a sweet disposition he had, how he liked cats. He had taken cooking to try to make good.

"It doesn't seem fair," Waldo said, "that someone should die trying. If you're going to die trying, what's the use of trying?"

"Right," said Wasserman, agreeing with one hundred percent of what Waldo had said, "and that's got nothing to do with psychology either. No sir. That's life."

Wasserman stopped giving Waldo advice. He gave him books instead. Waldo found that he could not finish the books, although when he started he was always interested in them. Part way through each one he became familiar with the characters, the style, the words even. Then they bored sweet hell out of him. It always added up to the same thing: the person with the problem either solved the problem and died, or died before he solved it. The point was in the dying. Dying was everything: the death itself and the fits and what did he say and what did he do just before he slipped off to deposit that rag of a soul in whatever heavenly laundry he might believe in. Of course, between the little sweats of youth and the wobbly shrieks of old age there were side trips and excursions and enough agony and ecstasy to turn the book into a huge bitching bundle of paper.

Waldo became a model prisoner. He started his own prison weekly called *Bars None*, wrote poems about what does it all mean and why is a tree and if the screws are the men in the gray-flannel suits then isn't Booneville the world? There were also his stories: each story started off all right (the boy falls in love, girl runs her hands over her breasts and discovers she is a woman) but they always ended with (1) a scream or (2) dead silence or (3) statements such as "Benny ran as fast as his little legs would carry him to the throbbing little piece called Muriel" or "You mean *you're* the one that fixed the plug that lit the room when I looked up and saw you standing naked . . . " etc. And there was the poem, "Dirge for a Sensitive Young Man" —

> *A shiny window fell on a boy,*
> *Pain is not something to enjoy;*
> *He tried to get out of the kitchen*
> *And maybe that was a sin,*
> *But he didn't know if he was out or in.*
> *Spare us all from being outside,*
> *Or if it's nice there, give me a ride.*

Several weeks later it was time to go. Wasserman said he was sorry to see Waldo go, but that he expected Waldo to visit his office as soon as he got home. He said he might have a few ideas for Waldo; maybe college. Warden Deed said now Waldo could see the world and, confidentially, good luck, son. Otto Noon said no shit. Erratio Lizardi said nothing, drooled. Waldo shrugged. It was time to go.

Standing just inside the glass at the Main Entrance to the Booneville School for Delinquent Boys Waldo did not have to fight back tears. Going gave him a good feeling, as if just on the other side of the next hill was a fortune to be made in something like garbage or true confessions. Going always seemed more profitable than staying.

"Who's going to pick you up?"

"My father."

Chapter Two

"See you later," Waldo's father said to the man in the gray uniform at the gate.

Waldo sat in the right front seat of the car picking at the frayed straw of the seat cover. He looked up in time to see the sign NEW LIFE LANE disappear past the window. Waldo's father ground the gears twice in a row trying to gain momentum on the pitted road.

Waldo's father was talking. He seemed to have been talking for a long time, but Waldo remembered that he had just picked him up at Booneville and that he had been in the car only ten minutes. His father kept talking, and although Waldo's home was not too far from Booneville his father was saying "it's no disgrace" for the third or fourth time.

Waldo's father cut into the left lane and forced a whining blue Pontiac into his wake of exhaust fumes. The cars beeped, honked, and lurched irate in a knot behind Waldo's father who was now straddling two lanes and traveling at ten miles below the speed limit.

"I know," Waldo said, examining a long strand of hemp and wondering why it had been painted with red stripes. "I've paid my debt."

"Why, you've paid your debt," Waldo's father said, ignoring his son's similar comment.

"I left it all behind me," Waldo said.

"Booneville is *all behind you*, son," Waldo's father said,

continuing at his own pace. "Now, I'm gonna tell you something you prolly never . . . "

"If it's about Uncle Walter," Waldo said, trying to be inoffensive, but failing to jar his father's hearing.

" . . . everybody liked . . . no, *loved* — everybody loved your Uncle Walter. Although that girl he was going around with was queer as a two-cent stamp." Waldo's father cursed the man ahead of him and then mumbled and narrowed his eyes at the rear-view mirror. After a while he continued, "And he — Walter — was *away* for quite some time — longer than fourteen measly months, I know that much. So you got *nothing in the world* to be ashamed of. Just remember what I told you about your Uncle Walter."

"I think I remember Old Uncle Walter," Waldo said.

"Course, that was long before your time," Waldo's father said. "He went in the Navy and jumped ship."

"Jumped ship?"

"What?"

"He *jumped ship* to an island and escaped?"

"No, he jumped ship to the water. Walter jumped off the back of the boat during a fire drill — with everybody watching. He drowned."

"I don't really blame him for jumping if the ship was lousier than the water," Waldo said. Then he added, "I can't see why everyone liked him so much. I really can't."

"Your mother's brother, Walter. Your mother." Waldo's father winced, then continued in a pained tone of voice, as if he were suffering physically from a wound which Waldo could not see. "Your mother. She used to cry all the time, Waldo. I mean, *very frequently* — if you get my meaning. But pretty soon she got used to the idea . . ." His voice trailed off.

"What idea?" Waldo said.

" . . . and pretty soon she didn't mind when I told people you were away. I always said, 'Waldo's away' — I figured they'd think you were at camp."

"For *fourteen months?*" Waldo asked, looking out the window at a swamp.

"Yes, Waldo, your mother used to cry. Like she did when you poured the molasses into her penny bank. She cried just like that. You remember how she cried when your poured molasses into her bank?"

Waldo tore out a fistful of hemp.

"I mean, why did you have to go and pour molasses into her penny bank? You know she was saving up for Rainy Day Galoshes with fur on the top edge. You didn't have to go and pour molasses into the bank. You know we love you an awful lot — we don't have to *tell* you that, do we, son?"

"No, Dad," Waldo said.

"So why'd you have to pour the molasses into it? You *knew* she was saving up. You know how women are when they're saving up?"

"I don't know, Dad," Waldo said. "I knew she was saving up, though."

"You should know better than that," Waldo's father said. "We've *tried* to teach you the right thing. God knows. They can't blame us," Waldo thought he heard his father mumble to some colored plastic statuary magnetized to the dashboard.

"No one's trying to blame you," Waldo said.

"They always say it's the parents' fault. Well, I say it's *not*. Simple as that. We do our best. They always say it's the parents' fault, though, don't they?"

"I've gotta get some smokes," Waldo said. "Stop when you get a chance, okay?"

"How many times have I told you not to smoke? I would really like to know how many times. It turns your teeth and

lungs and even your stomach *brown*. Besides, only Mau-
Maus smoke — you know that." He pulled the car over to
the curb and faced his son. The blinking neon sign of the
drugstore made his face flash on and off, red and pale, like a
bulb.

Waldo watched his father's blinking face with fascination.
It was one of the few times Waldo had ever really looked at
his father. And when I decide to finally look, thought Waldo,
I discover that he's not my father at all. He's a lamp! Waldo
laughed.

"What are you laughing at, Waldo? Not Mau-Maus, I
hope. Mau-Maus ain't too funny when they're living next
door to you throwing beer cans on your lawn and working like
hell to bring the valuation down on your property. Not too
funny, I'd say." Then he paused and said, "Get me a newspaper, Waldo."

"A paper?"

"Yeah, that's right, a *paper*, a *news*paper. I can't say anything wrong, can I, Waldo? I said, *can I?*"

"You do all the time."

"I mean, to *you*."

"That's what I mean."

But it was too late. Waldo's father had forgotten what he
had said. He knew he wanted to shout at Waldo; he was sure
of that. But the words had slipped out of his flashing head
and left only anger.

"Were there any Mau-Maus in Booneville, son?"

"Lots of them. Millions."

"I might have known," Waldo's father said.

Waldo returned to the car with the cigarettes and the newspaper.

"How much they cost you?" Waldo's father asked.

"Thirty."

"Ain't that Harold a sonofabitch about prices. Thirty for

smokes, eight and a half for a new truss. Someone someone should fix Harold's ass on straight. They ought to anyway. Why, that's highway robbery."

Waldo lit a cigarette and blew his mouthful of smoke in the direction of his father.

Waldo's father gasped on the smoke and said, "I know it must have been rough on you, Waldo, being up in that place with all those black Mau-Maus and things. You didn't write much, though. I told your mother they kept you busy with the number plates and stuff like that."

"We didn't make number plates, Dad," Waldo said.

"Well, your Uncle Walter used to make number plates. He made one that said *Walter*, his name you see? When he got out of the clink they arrested him for having *it* on his car instead of the regular one. Walter always did nutty things like that. Made everyone laugh, Walter did. He used to stomp Mau-Maus when he was a kid."

"We didn't make number plates."

"You didn't make number plates, eh? Did you make," Waldo's father snuffled and laughed; it looked as if he would not be able to get the last word out; then he said it, *"cars?"*

Having at last said the word Waldo's father thumped the steering wheel and laughed unashamedly and repeated his little joke as he snuffled ("If you didn't make number plates, did you make *cars?"*).

Waldo decided to let his father enjoy his joke. He said nothing. When his father stopped laughing he looked at Waldo again and asked him, for Pete's sake, what did he do all the time if he didn't make number plates?

Waldo thought a moment about the Booneville Gin he had helped make. It was too long a story to tell. "We saw the doctor and told him stories about our families."

"You told stories. You didn't *make up* stories, did you, Waldo?"

"Sure. I made them up."

"Did they make you do it?"

"No. It was easier than telling the truth."

"Which was?"

"Which was a lot of crap if you ask me."

Waldo looked at his father and noticed his face flashing red from the sign. The color was funny, but Waldo knew that it was still his father's face under it all and it didn't seem funny any more. *"Just what do you mean when you say that, boy! I'd like to know!"*

"Take it easy," Waldo said," smoking quietly.

"I *am* taking it easy — in case you weren't looking. Now I'd like to know why you made up stories about your family. I'd like to know why, that's all! You hear me?"

"All right. I'll tell you why," Waldo said, crushing his cigarette and letting the smoke trickle from his nostrils.

"So tell."

"I didn't want to tell them that you say the same thing to me about five hundred times so I told them you drink yourself into a sewer every night and I didn't want to tell them that Ma saves pennies and has one eye that doesn't look at me so I told them she beats me up every Tuesday afternoon when she comes home from the racetrack."

"You told them that?"

"Right. That's what I told them."

"What did they say?"

"They made me draw more pictures and tell more stories. So I did. It was easy, if you ask me."

"I should break every bone in your body," Waldo's father said, grinding back into first gear and sludging back into the traffic.

"Say it again," said Waldo.

"You've got a nerve talking to me like that. You ever notice that? You got a nerve . . ."

"You got a nerve being my father," Waldo said. "Or anyone else's for that matter. All men got nerves being their
sons' fathers. Kids should have doctors instead of fathers,
if you ask me."

Waldo's father was silent.

"Course, I'm the only son you got," Waldo said.

"Don't you realize," Waldo's father said, assuming the
pain-of-the-unseen-wound tone of voice, "you're the only
son we got. The only one. I'd like to know the number of
times I nearly gave you a damn good licking and then asked
myself, *Ed, he's the only son you got and you want to lick
him?* And then I'd answer myself: *Ed . . . you're bats.*
No, I never licked you once, did I? I wouldn't do a thing like
that. You're my only son — why should I lick you? You'll
get everything I have someday, every single thing. You'll in-
herit everything. Even though you've been away — we all
know that — now you're home with your dad. A kid's best
friend, his dad," Waldo's father said thoughtfully, "although
mine was the biggest sonofabitch Christ ever created, God
forgive me, rest his soul."

After a long pause Waldo's father said, "It's all yours —
everything I have. You're my hair."

Waldo tried to turn away but he found he could only turn
his head while the rest of his body faced the flat road almost
in agreement. When he turned he saw his reflection in the
side window. The face in the side window looked unhappy.
It made Waldo unhappy to look at the face, so finally he
turned his head back to where it was.

His father continued: ". . . I know it was rough up
there in Booneville. You don't have to tell me. God knows,
Walter near went crazy with the number plates and stuff.
Musta been the same thing with you. I don't blame you,
I guess, for telling all them crazy stories."

"It wasn't bad. It wasn't good. It was." Waldo thought a moment. "It wasn't bad. At least you could *do* things."

"You call lying about your parents *doing* something."

"I wasn't lying."

"What *did* you do, son? I keep asking myself, *what did you do?*"

"We didn't *blab* all the time, like *you're* doing!"

"Is there something wrong with blabbing, Waldo? Is that a sin?"

"Probably not. And maybe that's the trouble."

"Sure, you didn't know what you were doing," Waldo's father moaned. "Getting beat up all the time, I suppose. And those Mau-Maus didn't help things either."

Waldo thought of Otto Noon. He felt sorry for him a moment, and then Waldo envied him, Otto, being in a nice safe jail, a pen. Waldo wanted to change places with Noon. Let Noon sit in the front seat of his father's car and try to turn away. But Noon was still saying no shit and he had a concussion. "Niggers aren't so bad."

"Aren't so bad? Did you say *niggers aren't so bad?*"

"I know one. He's not so bad."

"Did you say *niggers aren't so bad?*"

"You're goddamned right I said niggers aren't so bad! I'll say it again if you want!" Waldo exploded.

"I wish, son," Waldo's father began quietly, "I really wish your mother could hear you now. She'd die if she could hear you using that kind of language. I know she'd die. *What's wrong with you, Waldo? What is wrong?*"

"Why don't you listen? Maybe if you'd listen once or twice I wouldn't have to holler and you wouldn't have to die listening to that kind of language. It only takes listening to hear, you know. And you want to know what's wrong with blabbing. *That's* what's wrong with blabbing!"

"*Listen?* To *what?* You want me to listen to you making wise remarks because your poor old mother's optic nerve rotted away when she was five years old?"

"She should have rotted away with it. Then this whole thing wouldn't have happened."

"You want me to listen to you saying smart things because your mother saves pennies in a nice old bank which *you poured molasses into?* I thought you were supposed to be *cured* and come home and all. You want me to *listen* to you? As if putting up with you wasn't enough! Why don't you crawl off with all your Mau-Mau friends."

"Maybe I will."

"You should."

"You're goddamn right I goddamn should."

"*Stop that!*"

Waldo lit another cigarette and then looked out the window. Outside a pregnant woman was wheeling a baby carriage. Waldo stared hard at the woman and then mumbled and shook his head.

"What?" Waldo's father asked.

"You can drop me here," said Waldo. "I'll be home later."

Chapter Three

It was dark when Waldo started home. The bus had stopped running and he had to walk the whole distance from town. On the way he met a man. The man walked along with him. Waldo commented on the sky; it was getting cloudy and gray, he said. The man said that life was really funny that way and it was no use to grumble. You had to smile, live, learn and remember that every dog had his day. And then the man put his arm around Waldo.

Waldo pulled away from the man and ran the rest of the way home. He spotted his house. It was made out of wood. It had stone steps now, but there had been wooden steps when he was sent to Booneville. There was a new ash can in front, too. Times change. The house stood still and dead, a dry wooden house on an empty street. A new ash can. The front of the house, clapboards and peeling paint, looked like the face of the man that had put his arm around him. The screen door hung open as if it was saying, "Life's really funny that way." A piece of cotton was stuck in a large hole that had rusted out.

All the lights were out. The family had gone to bed. They always went to bed before ten because Waldo's father's motto was, "The sleep you get after midnight is no good for you."

His suitcase stood in the middle of the room. Waldo went over and lifted it. It was still full. He put it over against the wall, still packed, and went up to bed.

He could not sleep. He rolled and tossed for hours on the bed. Out of sheer boredom he sat up and tried to discern his father's wheezing from his mother's light snoring. Then he tuned his ears past those two sounds and tried to hear Grammy's long laryngeal flutters. It took almost an hour but, in between the snores of his parents and the creaking of the walls, he managed to pick out a few. Grammy's flutters sounded like a death rattle. Waldo thought about that phrase a moment and pictured a little baby in a crib crying. He quiets down when his dad hands him a brand-new death rattle.

He went to sleep for short periods, but woke up for good when he saw the night lift and lighten and the dawn slowly sharpen itself on the window. The first sound he heard was from Grammy's room. He heard clattering and paper wrinkling. Grammy's breathing was very loud as she limped heavily past his room. He ducked under the covers when she went past so he never saw Grammy pause to peer into his room, her eyes glazed with sleep and age, brandishing her big knife, holding the twisted top of her paper bag like the neck of a dead hen.

She went downstairs and banged out the front door.

Waldo waited a moment and then crept downstairs. He spotted the penny bank and picked it up, pried off the bottom, took out the pennies and replaced them with some nuts and bolts he found in a cigarbox. Then he hammered the bottom back and put the penny bank in its usual place.

The bus driver was not happy to take the twenty loose pennies that Waldo spilled into his hand. But he took them when the man in back of Waldo said, "Money's money, I don't see what the fuss is all about."

Waldo rode downtown to Wasserman's office and stood in front. He was about to enter when he remembered that he had not seen his mother; it would not be fair to judge everything at home by the fruitless talk with his father or, for that matter, by the new ash can. He would have to see his mother. He was ashamed to spend the pennies on the bus so again he walked home, threw open the front door and said, "Here I am."

"Howdy do, Waldo!" The voice came from the kitchen.

Something inside Waldo, alerted by the snap of the voice, went dead with a sigh. He heard the clank of pans being dropped into the sink. And there she was.

"What did you say, son?" the woman asked. The woman looked at Waldo, but only with her face and one of her eyes. The other eye — the left one — drifted off and focused lazily on a wax tulip that stuck sharply from a sepia photograph of a uniformed Civil War officer. Or it might have been another war. The woman could never remember, since it was her cousin and not her father or brother.

"You didn't see Grammy when you were out, did you? Say, Waldo, you lost weight! You come right in here and have something to eat. Why, landsakes, you're all skin and bones!"

"You were just wondering if I saw Grammy?" Waldo remained on the sofa.

"Yes. You didn't, did you? See her?"

"No," said Waldo. "I've been in prison."

"I didn't think you would."

"She won't lose her way back."

"She's in Oak Grove, son. You know that. So why do you have to talk that way about someone who loves you?"

"I wonder what Doctor Wasserman would say if I told him I had a grandmother that hunted dandelions in a cemetery all day," said Waldo. "He'd go nuts."

"All I know is, your Grammy's a pretty smart cookie for

her age," the woman said knowingly. "Which is over seventy, I imagine. And she still has a lot of I-don't-know-what in her."

"I don't know either," said Waldo.

"That Willy Czap passed away yesterday. The one that shrunk. You know the Czaps, you know Sybil Czap. The poor thing!"

"I was in prison."

"They say you just couldn't look at him near the end — horrible and eaten away, I imagine." She paused to wipe her hands on her apron. It was a large white apron, the kind people wear when they deal in cuts of meat. She looked out the window and continued. "I heard them going by on their way to Oak Grove, the Czaps. Cadillacs and everything. They had wreaths a mile a minute — never saw so many in my whole life. All sorts of designs, too, and colors. A regular garden they had in them cars, I'm telling you. They did it up in grand style." The woman mumbled, "grand style" several more times before the boy spoke.

"So they buried him at Oak Grove, eh?"

"You can't take it with you," the woman said quickly, without emphasis. She did not smile.

"No," said Waldo.

"Anyway, it must have let them all in. The dogs, you know. The dogs always chase those funeral things right through the front gate of Oak Grove. Grammy'll be mad as a hen."

"What do dogs have to do with Grammy digging dandelions?" Waldo asked, showing some interest.

"Well," the woman said, pursing her lips into a mocking smile, shaking her head from side to side, and closing one of her eyes, "I know I'd be *pretty careful* about eating dandelions that grew in a place where dogs were. Because dogs," she smiled, "just might have done you-know-what on them. I'm telling you I'd be mighty careful."

"So would I," said Waldo, trying to be unconvincing.

"Your Grammy's careful where she picks her dandelions. And she's very *scientific* about it. I mean she makes a regular study of dandelion picking and digging. Always did, your Grammy."

"Swell," said Waldo.

"But, *dogs!* Why, my land, there must have been hundreds of them following that Czap procession to Oak Grove. Poor old Grammy, she probably spent the whole day smelling dandelions and chasing dogs."

"She doesn't mind dogs. She raised one herself for fifty years," said Waldo glancing up at his mother.

"Oh, we always had a dog. We all had a feeling for dogs — and rats and mice, too. All kinds of animals just flocked to our house. But dogs — they can smile at you." The woman smiled. "Or growl." The woman growled. "I always said I'd rather have a person growl at me than a dog. Dogs mean it ever so much more."

"She works like one," Waldo sighed. "Like a dog."

The woman was now looking at two parts of the ceiling instead of two of the wall. "I imagine Grammy's just sitting there pleased as punch with all that grass and flowers and music. She does it every day."

"Well, I was in the pen every day."

"Stop complaining, Waldo. That's all you know how to do. I wouldn't mind, but you actually *look* for things to complain about."

"I don't have to look far. I just have to use both my eyes."

"You never complained when you were small. I never remember you beefing about a thing. You were a nice little boy. I always said, that Waldo's going to be a gentleman when he grows up to be a big boy. All I can say is, what happened? You're supposed to be grown up and look! Your father says you're all cured and nice and you start in complaining. You call that cured?"

"I graduated from the pen. I must be cured."

"What did they teach you there, Waldo? Did they teach you to beef and be a wiseacre? I tell you, some day, some sunny day, you're going to push me too far and I'll beat you to within an inch of your life! I swear to God in Heaven as my witness, Waldo."

The woman sat down in a straight-backed chair, put her head in her hands and moaned, hunching her shoulders jerkily — the way some people laugh. But tears were running between her fingers and plopping onto her lap. "You're cured, my eye! The least you could to when you talk to your mother," she sobbed, "is keep a civil tongue in your cheek!"

"I'm just trying to tell you about Booneville, the pen."

"Don't tell *me* what they teach you in jail. I heard all about it from your Uncle Walter and it was no bed of roses either. Don't you dare tell me a thing, Waldo. You forget I'm your mother. Oh, I know how badly you want to get my goat — "

"Who wants *your* goat — "

Waldo's mother leaped into the air and faced Waldo. She hopped over to him and stooped like a gargoyle, "See! you *do* hate me, Waldo! I knew it would come out! I could *kill* you. Don't give me the chance, please don't give me the chance or I *will* kill you!"

"Now, no one's going to kill anyone around here!" The voice rasped through the screen door. "Although someone should get a damn good hiding."

An old woman came through the door and slammed it shut so hard that the wad of cotton flew out of the rusted hole and settled on the porch. The woman was carrying a paper bag, overstuffed, in one clenched fist and a long knife upraised in the other fist. The knife dropped clods of dirt onto the linoleum. She stood eagle-like a moment, her claws full. Then she wheeled and squawked at Waldo's whimpering mother. Waldo's mother was still recovering from the frenzy which had congealed and been deposited into a balled-up handkerchief clutched tightly in her hand. "Let's be reasonable," the woman said, her feet planted firmly on the floor, "so's we can at least carry out our threats instead of letting them hang in the air. And for godsakes, don't get all riled up over *that* mound." She jerked the knifeblade in the direction of Waldo, flinging a cube of dirt at his abdomen.

"Who are you calling a mound?" Waldo asked, looking up at the beak for the first time and seating himself.

"I'm calling *you* a mound, and get off your butt when there's a lady present. Didn't they teach you that along with the toothbrushing lessons?"

"You've been *listening*, Mother," the younger woman said.

"You're damn right I've been listening," the eagle said. "I've been out on those steps for ten minutes. I came in to throw up."

"*Mother*, Waldo can *hear* you!"

"Well, I had to listen to him. I'm sick. Leave me alone. I should've stayed in Oak Grove — it was quiet once Czap and his noisy bunch took off."

"How'd the hunting go?" asked Waldo.

"Yes, Mother, how *did* the dandelion-hunting go? Did you get an awful lot of them?"

"Emma, will you stop talking to me like that! You're *my* daughter, remember? You don't have to use that baby talk until I start using it. Which will be never I hope."

"Dogs?" asked Waldo.

"Not many," said Grammy. "Willy Czap brought some

with him. You know, they were chasing his casket. I never liked the kid anyway. I like him even less now."

"No one'll miss that nasty little Willy Czap," said the younger woman into space.

"Emma, don't say that. This is no laughing matter. A lot of people will miss him. What difference does it make what he was like before? When he's dead he's dead and you know it." Grammy was out of breath. She moistened her lips and went on. "His family might miss him, don't you think so? I said don't you think — "

"I heard what you said. You also said you didn't like him."

"Doesn't mean a thing. You can hate a person and still miss him. In fact, if he goes off and dies and lets a million dogs in with his casket to pee on the dandelions, then I'd say he's really put one over on you. Wouldn't you say so, Waldo?"

"Eating dandelions? Peed-on or not I wouldn't eat them."

"You better wise up, Waldo. Dandelions kept me afloat during the depression. I owe a lot to dandelions. And you owe a lot to me." Grammy narrowed her eyes and said without moving her lips, "and don't you ever forget it."

"You're just tired, Grammy, that's all. Why don't you . . ."

"*Tired?* Why, it's restful sitting there with those stones. I can hardly wait to be put there under six feet of nice heavy dirt. And when I finally get shoveled into that hole *you're going to miss me.* And so are you, Waldo. Let's get that straight right now."

"Of course, Grammy. We'll miss you to death," the woman said. "You've been so nice to us."

"I *bore* you and six others like you!" Grammy thundered.

"We don't mind," said Emma.

"Emma," said Grammy panting and looking around, "I was an old-fashioned housekeeper once, before you were born, before anyone was born around here. Lived in this house, too, and I was very happy with my chicken fat and my apple pandowdies. I went to church and sang 'Holy, Holy, Holy' and made the best fritters in the church bazaar. I was tough as a whalebone corset, steady as a clock, busy as a little bee and cheerful as a cricket. I could dish up good advice and home cures like lumpy oatmeal. I was a good neighbor and friend, with a bottle of hooch in the pantry and a heart of gold. I was the local midwife with strong clean hands and I gave birth and saw all this," she gestured around the room, "into the world. The mangy sofa, your hair-dryer and Quikee Dinners, disposals, electric toothbrushes, snow-loaders, and green stamps and, my God, a grandson, pulled out of you with steel tongs, crazy as a loon and a jailbird to boot!"

"Mother," said Waldo's mother, "you sad thing!"

"My God," said Grammy in bald despair.

"I try," said Waldo's mother.

"Everybody tries."

"Not you, Waldo," said Grammy, "or you either, Emma."

"You're always picking at us, Grammy."

"It's picking *on* us, not picking *at* us," said Waldo.

"This is it, by God," said Grammy. "I'm getting out of here."

"I need a vacation — I'm coming with you," said Waldo.

"No," said Grammy. "If I'm going to my Maker I'm going alone. I hate crowds. I hate this mob!" She looked at Waldo and then at her daughter and said, "You will *let* me, won't you?"

Waldo's mother crooked her arms in the air and twitched them over the heads of Grammy and Waldo. "Go!" she shrieked. "Both of you can go to . . . to . . ."

"SAY IT EMMA I DARE YOU!" shouted Grammy.

"Blazes!" Waldo's mother blubbered.

"I won't need these," said Grammy pitching the dandelions into the wastebasket across the room.

"For Godsakes," said Waldo.

"I'm going off to die," said Grammy. "This is a nut-house."

"They call them funny farms," said Waldo. "That's what this is." A song title occurred to Waldo: "How're You Going To Keep Them Down On The Funny Farm After They've Seen Booneville?"

"My God," said Grammy.

Waldo's mother was still tensed, rigid, her feet apart. She began waving her arms in tight little squares above her head. She screamed breathlessly, "You think you're the only ones that are persecuted. You think Edwin and I have it easy. Well, let me tell you, you're just as wrong as you can be!" She trembled and sweat in Grammy's direction, then in Waldo's. She finally said to the wall, "I don't have it easy. I'm going all the time. Just going and going!"

"I'm going now," sighed Grammy placing her cutlass on the coffee table.

"Nobody has it easy," said Waldo. "But some people have it harder than others."

"What do you know about having it *hard*?" asked Grammy. She put her face close to Waldo's and waited for an answer. Her big-beaked face, close-up, was soft, wrinkled as if it were slowly becoming food, becoming edible. "When I was a girl I had it hard. I worked in a factory."

"They don't have factories any more."

"What do you know about that?" sneered Grammy.

"I know plenty. I can see, you know. That helps."

Waldo's mother began nodding furiously, nuttily. "I know, I *know*. That's meant as a wisecrack to me. I'm not stupid . . . or as stupid as you think I am."

"No one accused you of being *stupid*, exactly," said Grammy, tiredly. "But I've done my bit. I'm leaving now . . . maybe for good. I hope the house corrodes. I hope I die. I hope the dogs leave the cemetery. I am *living on hope*." Grammy shuffled out of the living room, slamming the screen door. She limped down the long, cracked walk, one shoulder higher than the other.

Waldo's mother continued, ". . . so this is a looney bin, is it? Well, you live here and so does she." Waldo's mother jerked her thumb toward the screen door. "So what does that make you? I'm not the only nut around here, I know that much; I *know* I *couldn't* be the only nut around here. Or this whole place wouldn't be a looney bin. There has to be someone else."

"It's not me," said Waldo.

"Then, it's her," said Waldo's mother, just raising her thumb this time, as if the thumb had now become Grammy.

"Okay, maybe it is," said Waldo to the thumb, "as long as it ain't me."

"Well, I think it *is* you, Waldo. Anyone can *see* how you've changed."

Waldo mumbled a reply.

"You hear me, Waldo? Why aren't you looking at me? I swear I am learning to hate this house." She paused. "And I am learning to hate you, Waldo. Talk about dogs in cemeteries! Why, this whole place is going to the dogs! Waldo . . . look me in the eye and I will tell you you've been an awful disappointment to me and to Grammy and especially to your father."

"I've already explained the whole thing to him."

"Look at me when you speak to me," said Waldo's mother.

"I'm looking," said Waldo.

"You're *not* looking!"

"I'm looking as much as I ever wanted to look," said Waldo.

"LOOK ME IN THE EYE!" screamed Waldo's mother.

Waldo went over to the knife on the coffee table. He picked it up and walked to a window box which was resting on the sill and several thicknesses of newspapers. Then he lopped five geraniums and left them hanging from the sides of their pots as if they were nauseated. Waldo kicked over the wastebasket with the dandelions in it and spilled everything in it onto the linoleum. Walking past his mother he said, almost in a whisper, "your eye" and continued into the kitchen, slamming the door behind him. He flicked on the disposal and tried to force the knife into it.

In the living room Waldo's mother stood quiet a moment surveying the room intently with her good eye. With the kind of determination that her mother must have had in the days when she was tough as a whalebone corset she walked over to the window boxes.

As Waldo entered the living room again he saw his mother bent over the right side of the window box pushing the stems of the cut geraniums back into the dirt.

Chapter Four

Doctor Wasserman was a general practitioner, trained as an optometrist, but now indulging in therapy. He worked part-time at Booneville because Warden Deed had a theory about criminals. He thought it was their eyes that caused all the trouble: rapists squinted, the eyes of a thief bulged, masturbators sported circles. He hired Wasserman to test everyone's eyes. As it turned out, Waldo was one of the few boys at Booneville who did not need glasses. Wasserman analyzed the boys as they identified the small print on the eyecharts in the darkness. "Tell me about yourself," Wasserman would say as he fitted one lens and then another over the boy's eyes.

He also had an office in town and although the sign outside said he was an eye doctor everyone in town knew he was a headshrinker. So after leaving his mother to her hacked geraniums Waldo went to Wasserman's office. He remembered that he was supposed to let the doctor know how things were going at home.

He went into the waiting room and started reading a medical magazine. When he saw the pictures of the woman with the sores on her breast (before) which were cured (after) by regular treatment with a drug he could not pronounce, he closed the magazine, dropped it and looked up.

The waiting room was decorated in a jungle motif: pots of ivy, ferns, a vase of hardy mums and a jungle painting which, when Waldo squinted at it, was not of rare trees and

flowers, but of millions of people with their arms outstretched like branches and red angry faces like lovely blossoms. There was also a painting with a texture like tooth-
paste squeezed directly from the tube; perfect for a dentist's
office. Waldo reflected on the pictures: the only pictures
that ever mattered to him were not in art galleries but in
filthy homes and doctors' offices.

But something else added a certain brightness to the room.
In the farthest corner sat some colors or, rather, a woman
wearing some colors. It was her white knee-length coat, her
ochre hat and gloves, her red toreador slacks and her straw
shoes with fruit on them that made her look as if she were
dangling rather than sitting. The colors pulsed.

The woman was filling an ash tray with bits of a magazine
and then blasting the pile of paper with a cigarette lighter
which shot a long flame. She cheerfully added more paper
and lit it all. Waldo sniffed at the burning paper and the
smell of lush plants. He thought of jungle warfare.

When the woman saw him watching her she got up and
moved across the room toward him. She was what is known
as statuesque, but with a little of the carnival still lingering
about her, elegant and fleshy. The kind of elegance that cre-
ates silence. Give Nefertiti an ochre hat and you've got it.
An orchid sprouted from her left breast. The woman seemed,
as it were, rich.

The woman sat down next to Waldo, rather close and
crushing the orchid against Waldo's arm. She said hello
sweetly and smiled in a way that did not seem to match the
wild colors and strong flowery odors she carried with her.

Waldo returned the greeting.

The woman smiled again by just the slightest curl of her
very red lips and she continued smiling. Unlike the loud
clothes the smile was silent, certain, like Motherhood or the
Right Answer. Like the smile that appears quietly from

many figures in a bank book. From what Waldo could see of the woman's body it looked, as they say in novels, firm, supple, tawny, taut when it is stroked, and so forth. In the center of the woman's eyes was a sparkle that seemed to come from somewhere within her lovely head. The eyes were not smiling with the mouth. They were sensitive lenses that told the mouth to smile.

The clownish aspects of the woman, the clothes, the shoes with tiny fruit on them, were forgotten when Waldo looked at her eyes and imagined how much money it must have cost the woman to maintain the peace that he saw in them. He did not notice that his fingers were pressing gently against the woman's white coat or that his whole right leg was flipping up and down nervously. Waldo tried to think of something intelligent to say. He thought of nothing.

The woman asked Waldo if he needed glasses. He said no. She said she didn't think he did, that no one really needed glasses, that most people — her, for example — felt their way around. It was more fun, feeling. Wasserman was a feeler, a frustrated shrink, but a feeler.

"You known him long?" asked Waldo.

"Too long. He's become sort of an investment. I've poured money into him until I think he's going to break out in blotches — each blotch the size of a half-dollar, like they say. But these things will *actually contain* half-dollars. You know? He probably isn't human enough to break out in a skin disease, though. A bank is more like it. Shrinks are banks. When I was a little girl I had a bank that you put pennies into. Whenever a penny dropped into its stomach a little *thank you* sign appeared for about two seconds in its mouth — it was a gorilla. You'd have to put in another penny to get the sign again. I used to get a big kick out of putting money in it — it became human when money hit it. Wasserman is just the opposite. You put the money in and he turns into a bank that listens to how I tried to freeze a gallon of my husband's martinis with liquid oxygen. Wasserman, like the true bank he is, points out that I hate my husband — a fact that I've known since the day I found some nude pictures in his desk drawer. But Wasserman has certainly been around and he reaches conclusions very quickly. He has a textbook with two pages in it — a very thin textbook of shrink. It has a rule of shrink on each page. One, *it's always people, and never places or things.* Two, *hateful things are done out of sheer hate and never any confusing emotion like love or lighting a cigarette.* It's sensible, but limited."

"It sounds sensible," said Waldo.

"All right, that's my theory after three years of observation. What's yours?"

"I don't know. I haven't known too many doctors — as a matter of fact Wasserman's the first one, unless druggists are doctors, which I doubt."

"Druggists." The woman paused before she pronounced sentence. "Druggists make hot fudge sundaes and sell . . . rubber life rafts, magazines, snow tires, bedpans, and unmentionables." The woman spoke as if she either had read it and remembered it or had said it on many other occasions. She went on. "I have this idea. They should take the old ladies that sell magazines and candy bars in the subway and put them in drugstores with big kettles and giant spoons. Then, they make this medicine in the kettle that will cure *anything,* like witches, you know? The ladies feed this stuff to the druggists and it turns them into toads that must spend the rest of their life hopping around trying to get to Israel, only they never will. I hate Jews."

Waldo looked at his knee. "I've known Doctor Wasserman fourteen months and one and a half days."

"You keep pretty close track."

"Everybody kept count where I was. Besides, we were reminded every so often."

"Where were you?"

"The pen."

"A jailbird! What'd they get you for? Anything good?"

"I don't know. I was seventeen when they arrested me. It was mostly stuff around the house. Stupid stuff. Fouling up my mother's bank and cutting her clothes line, and then burning my father's truss and pouring five gallons of motor oil into the hopper. And letting the air out of his tires." Waldo paused, his eyes half-closed, studiously as his mind whirred back fifteen months. "And there were some dirty pictures, like your husband's, I guess. But I don't hate anybody. That is, anybody that I know of — unless you can hate parts of people."

"*Parts* of people?"

"Like my father's stupid jaw — mostly his mouth. And especially my mother's eye. And my grandmother's lips have turned to wrinkles. But I don't hate them all over."

"So they sent you up for doing those crazy things?"

"Yes. Oh, I suppose if it was Hallowe'en or the Fourth of July I could've gotten out of it. Jokes, I could've said they were. I did them most in August and September."

"Those are pretty lousy months for alibis."

"The worst. September was really the worst. I didn't know it then, but I wasn't thinking about it either. I was on vacation in August so it seemed like a good time for burning the truss, and for the other stuff."

"What about September? Were you on vacation then?" The woman took a cigarette out of a box and inserted it into a long holder.

"Not really," said Waldo, "I did the stuff in September

because I was on vacation still, but I shouldn't have been. I didn't want to be on vacation in September. You're not *supposed* to be on vacation in September. I never was before — I was always in school."

The cigarette holder hindered the woman's *clucks* considerably.

"But after I graduated from high school I didn't go to college because of operations — like my old man's . . . pelvis, and my old lady's eye. Her optic nerve, they said. No money, said my old man. So I said to myself if I'm going to be on vacation I'm going to let him know I'm on vacation." Waldo paused. "After a while he got the point. He went to the police station — he could barely walk." Waldo stopped and smiled as he recalled the crablike walk of his father, the bones fusing overnight, and the hour it took to walk the painful three blocks to the police station to turn him in. "And he turned me in and they arrested me on charges of truss-burning, bank-screwing up, and oil-pouring."

"Really?" The woman asked, throwing her head back in genuine amusement. "Is that what they said?"

"No. That's what *I* said. And when I wrote it out and tried to give a speech at mess hall to the rest of the kids, the screws — that's what they called the guards at the pen — a good name, I think — got POed. That's how I met Wasserman."

"Free shrinking. What the hell," said the woman.

"I didn't think you had to pay for just talking."

"Maybe you don't. I've got to pay him plenty for the things I say. It figures."

"You pay him a lot, huh?"

"Not that much. I could lose it just as easy at the track. Maybe easier at the Heart Fund or something like that. I suppose if just *spending* money is therapy — and I think it is — then I'm on the road to recovery. Quite a long road, I might add. I've been on it for two years!" The woman's laughter was gentle.

"Well," said Waldo, "I've been on *vacation* for two years."

"That's something we've got in common. I spend," the woman nodded, "quite a bit of time on vacation come to think of it." She looked at Waldo, searching his face without effort with her soft eyes. Not unkindly, but not neglecting anything. Then her eyes widened and she pumped out, "I like fun." Her eyes, glassy with enthusiasm now, sparkled as she let the sounds of the last word die somewhere between her parted lips.

"I like fun too," said Waldo, thinking of the motor oil running in bubbly eddies in the toilet.

"I like to burn magazines," said the woman.

"I noticed," said Waldo, glancing at the smoldering ash tray.

"I like to say swears, too," said the woman.

"You do?" questioned Waldo, caught a bit off guard.

"Shit," said the woman, simply.

Waldo emitted something between a grunt and a chuckle.

"I know all of them. Some maybe you never heard of."

"Maybe," said Waldo, convinced, as the woman shaped her teeth and lips and pretended to say a word Waldo had never seen a woman show knowledge of.

"You don't look like the type," said Waldo. "That knows swears."

"I know everything," said the woman.

"Yes," replied Waldo sincerely.

"I do," said the woman not in protest. "I'm sensitive — especially to sensitive young men like you. I know you like to give speeches sometimes and pour oil in hoppers — I could tell before you told me so. I know how you feel about vacations. I feel the same way. I know you like to have *fun*. And so do I."

Waldo had already said, "I like your eyes," before he realized what the words actually meant.

"Thank you," said the woman. "You have very delicate hands, but your shoes are dirty. I know you have other things on your mind more important."

Waldo looked down and slid his shoes to the edge of the low chair slowly and as inconspicuously as possible. "I'm a slob," he said ingenuously. "I don't have many things on my mind. I guess I just enjoy being a slob."

"I don't blame you," said the woman, then she added cryptically, "you've got to be sort of a slob in this world or they'll kill you." She laughed. "I'm a slob myself. I have no bra on. Isn't that a scream?"

"It certainly — "

"Why worry?" the woman added slowly and with joy.

Waldo curled his lip and nodded in affirmation.

"You must think I'm a rather forward old lady," said the woman.

"No," Waldo returned. "Not at all. I like you — I mean I don't have any trouble talking to you."

"How old do you think I am?"

"Can't tell."

"You haven't tried. You answered too quickly. Go ahead — guess."

"I've been trying and I just can't figure it. In a way you're older than my mother, I think. I'm not too good on women's ages." Or much else for that matter, Waldo thought. "How old are you?"

"Thirty-seven tomorrow."

"My mother's fifty — fifty years old."

"I don't believe in being coy about ages. Tomorrow is my birthday. I have one every year — like everyone else. Only

I'm *Leo*." The woman was assured. "You are eighteen."

"I'll be nineteen next year."

"See, I was right. How's that? It's been a long time since I've sized up an eighteen-year-old boy. I'm not rusty, am I?"

"No," said Waldo, amazed.

"How'd you like to come to my birthday party?"

"I don't know."

"What do you *mean*, you don't know? After all I've told you. I've *confided* in you and you're going to do that to me!" For the first time since they had begun speaking the woman's face underwent a real change. Waldo did not like the change. "Don't let me down," she added.

"Okay."

"Okay what?" said the woman sitting forward slightly.

"Okay. I won't let you down."

"You know what that means, don't you?"

"What?" said Waldo.

"The party. You've got to come."

"All right," Waldo said, smiling when he saw the placid smile of the woman return. He wanted to go to the party. He might make a little money on it. He liked this woman, thirty-seven or not, what's the difference? And she wanted him to come to the party ("Don't let me down!"). Waldo peeked down her dress. It was just like in a novel.

"You're a doll," said the woman. "I'll meet you right here tomorrow at five."

"Okay," said Waldo.

The woman's expression did not change. It was still bright as she folded her gloves and started to rise. Her back was almost completely turned when Waldo told her that he didn't even know her name.

"I don't know yours either," said the woman.

"Waldo."

"Mine's Clovis."

Waldo was about to ask the woman her last name when the door to the inner office opened. A nurse's head appeared and said, "The doctor will see you now, Mrs. Techy."

Waldo had no control over what he did next. He said, very loudly and painfully distinct, *"Thanks a million!"*

"Five," was all Clovis Techy said, and she did not bother to turn. She had a large handbag that bumped against her long coat. She slid it up to her shoulder and wobbled into Wasserman's office on her straw-covered spikes. After the door slammed shut Waldo was sure he heard the high laughter of this grown woman.

Chapter Five

Good-bye Ma, hello Mrs. Techy. Waldo felt as if he had just been handed Life in a not-so-plain wrapper: fun on the inside, no return address, adults only. But Waldo was not sure what was in store for him. Mrs. Techy seemed a bit wacky, but she cared for him and spoke directly to him, listened to what he said. Waldo pictured himself introducing Mrs. Techy to his mother: Ma, I'd like you to meet Clovis Techy; Clovis, this is my Ma. And then as he grinned at his mother she would say, You bet your boots we're gonna raise a stink! Mrs. Techy would only smile.

And now it was Waldo's turn to see Wasserman and either get his eyes tested or his head examined. Waldo hoped he wouldn't start on all the God business. He had told Wasserman several times that God wasn't his red wagon or his family's either. They just weren't religious types. Although Grammy said my God all the time, although his father bought glow-in-the-dark religious items, Grammy wasn't praying and his father used the luminous virgins as night lights to the bathroom and to hang things on in the car. They were handy, Waldo's father said.

"Waldo," said Wasserman as Waldo entered the office, "how're you making out?" But Wasserman did not wait for an answer. He was on the phone. He held the phone in the crook of his neck and motioned for Waldo to take a seat.

The chair was large and leathery and wheezed as Waldo

sat. Wasserman was talking business. Waldo concentrated on a painting (a still life of a bagel and a cruller) and thought of Clovis Techy and then of his parents and Grammy and home, that is, the wooden house with the new ash can.

His mother's face appeared: she hounded him and told him that the place was going to the dogs. Waldo imagined a steel ball that leaves its pinball machine for fourteen months. It bounces back from Booneville into the chute and then is plunged into the usual routine: *whop*, it hits a bell, the bell rings; *blip*, a post, the ball bounces; *thlump*, it's flipped to a rubber band; *glik*, into a dancing man. It rattles around in a noisy box until, after being ejected from a hole or two, it drops with barely a sound into the dark trough near the coin slot.

He would have to get out again and move. Clovis seemed capable of moving things. Waldo was not sure why this was so, although he thought that money might have something to do with it. But the problem was not in just moving yourself, it was moving that other thing, that little dry house that roosted inside your chest, that place where some of the memories and all of the glands lived. People had a tendency to give the little dry house names like heart, soul, ego, which did not interest Waldo at all. He knew only that he would have to leave soon and in leaving he would have to lug the little house with him to give its occupants (memories, glands) a change of scenery. A new neighborhood was needed, that was all.

There was nothing bad about the old neighborhoods except that there was no future in them and no money to be made in them. The only pleasant thing was the hatred the old neighborhoods inspired in Waldo; he had learned to hate with edges, with style, almost without effort. There was safety in this and of course safety was the soil in which love could sprout and shoot up, become juicy and then seedy, and finally burst its pod and float out anger, disgust, jealousy, revenge.

But safety wasn't everything and when Waldo thought about it he decided that there wasn't any cash in it. He thought how easy it must have been for Grammy, no great lover of cash, in her factory, working sixteen, eighteen hours a day. Busy as a bee, cheerful as a cricket and steady as a clock, and buzzing, chirping and ticking in the same spot with no desire to move on. For Waldo the problem remained: where to cart that little dry house?

Waldo was brought back to the picture of the bagel and the cruller when Wasserman hung up the phone with a ring and a bang and rolled back in his swivel chair and asked Waldo what was up.

Waldo said not much. He talked about his mother's eye a bit, still blue, about the geraniums, how he tried to ram the knife into the disposal and blah-blah-blah . . .

"What *about* the disposal?"

Waldo reenacted the scene and narrated it. He finished with, ". . . and I stopped the thing cold."

"You stopped the thing *how?*"

"Cold," Waldo said. "That okay?"

"Okay? It's great! Yeah, I like that a lot. Right by the book." Wasserman scribbled some things down on a pad, unstuck his lips, sighed and then said, "I was just talking to a friend of mine at Rugg College. I was telling him you should be in college. You got smarts. Sure, you're not croaking because they're so big. But you got smarts."

"So I got smarts. What does that prove?"

"Watch it. Aggression."

"Well, what *does* it prove?"

"It doesn't prove anything technically. Not a thing. You

take your average slob. He's a slob. Right? But he's not a neurotic. Now, you're neither a slob nor a neurotic, unfortunately for me. But you're wasting your mother's good knives in her garbage disposal. You belong in college."

Waldo laughed. "I'll find something in college to foul up too. I get tired of the same neighborhoods and then I start nagging and leaving, looking for new neighbors."

"You want new neighbors? College is the place. Besides, look at it this way." Wasserman started counting on his fingers. "There's only a few things left for you. You've got to start making choices. Now, people don't run away from home to join the circus any more. You're too old to go steady and too young to get married." Wasserman stopped. What he had just said reminded him of a song and he didn't like it one bit. He continued. "You can't slave your ass off in a factory because there aren't any more factories, there aren't any paper routes, no ointment-selling, and you certainly can't sell Christmas cards — "

"Well, why do I have to *do* anything at all?"

Wasserman looked at Waldo closely. Waldo fidgeted.

"Say that again," said Wasserman.

"Well, do I? I mean, *have* to do something?"

"Oh boy," Wasserman whistled. "You got a lot to learn about life. Now life is not too easy. It's tricky. I would even say it's tough. But what you have to do — and I know this because I'm in the business — is *do* something, anything."

"Anything?"

"There are limits. A couple, I guess. Now what you have to realize is when you were most unhappy. When?"

"Was I most unhappy? I've never been really unhappy."

"That's your first lie."

"Okay. I was unhappy when I was at Booneville."

"The whole time?"

"No."

"Specifically when?"

"Specifically when I was in the infirmary."

"Doing what?"

"Getting better."

"Which means?"

"Nothing."

"Right. Go on."

"And I was unhappy at home, I think."

"You think? That's why you burned your father's truss, that's why you poured motor oil into the toilet and molasses into the penny bank? That's why you rammed a steak knife into the garbage disposal? You don't know whether you were unhappy or not? You're a peach."

"All right, so I was unhappy."

"You don't see any pattern here?"

"A small one."

"You're not that big, Waldo. A cootie like you can't screw up the universe. Now you just proved my point. If you don't do something, and if you don't do it fast, you're going to be buggy in a year. Every time you weren't doing something — even if that something was taking a crap — you were at large and you did the wrong thing. So my advice to you is make a friend, sell something, say something, go somewhere. Stop trying to live — life is too hard to live, so you have to do something else, keep your mind off life. That's a psychiatrist talking. And I've seen a hell of a lot of people come down the turnpike."

Waldo thought for a moment. His idea of changing neighborhoods seemed about the same as Wasserman's. But where to cart that little dry house?

"Okay, what do I do?"

"Hold on. Now I said paper routes, marriage and honest toil are all out. And you can't go steady. So I'm going to give you the same advice I'd give to any high school dropout or urban unemployable or drugstore cowboy: go to college. If you want to find yourself, find yourself at college."

"I'll go."

Wasserman said he had a friend at Rugg College, not too far away, a few hours by bus. He said that he had just called the President — an old friend by the name of Arnold Wermy — and fixed everything up. He would call again and tell him that Waldo should get on the list of accepted candidates. There might be a money problem, Wasserman added, but he winked and said, "Where there's spunk, there's money."

Waldo looked pleased. Moving once again. Then he said, "Say, Dr. Wasserman, what's a professional man?"

"It's a guy that does something for a profession like a doctor or a dentist or a lawyer."

"What about those people that work on newspapers? The ones that write the news. Are they professional men?"

"Good question," said Wasserman. He thought a moment. "You want to be a newspaper editor — reporter or something?"

"I thought about it. You remember I did a little writing at Booneville, the stories and the paper."

"If you want to be a professional man it's up to you. Just depends on how much you believe in your job, how much faith you have and how much money you make. If you've got faith — not a thing can stop you from being a professional man. Only, one thing. You say it wrong. It's not a professional *man*, it's a *professional* man."

"Sure," said Waldo. "Now what's the name of that college again?"

"Rugg," said Wasserman licking a cigar, still smiling across the desk at Waldo whose mouth was open at about the same angle as Wasserman's, but empty.

Waldo thanked Wasserman and told him he'd do his best. He knew it would be hard, but if Dr. Wasserman was willing to go to the trouble of getting him into college then he could at least give it a try. He certainly had no intention of returning to Booneville. You just didn't return. Waldo thought that all the moving around had proved one thing to him. Even though some things were good you still spent half your life discovering that most things you did were all wrong and that you would never do them again. What of the other half of life? Well, I'm not Grammy yet, thought Waldo.

Waldo was anxious to go to Rugg and meet Clovis and forget about his father, his mother and the rest. If you weren't a coward you could start a new life. It was just opening an unlabeled can and dumping the contents on your plate and taking a big spoonful of the stuff.

Dr. Wasserman wanted to know if there was anything else that had happened besides the knife. Anything that he should know. Anything that Waldo had on his mind.

A figure danced into Waldo's head. The figure was wearing a daffodil hat in ochre, gold gloves, a tentlike white chiffon coat and huge fruited shoes. The figure took off the coat and gloves. Underneath, the figure was wearing a costume made entirely of money. The figure plucked off the paper money costume gingerly and held out the pile of money to Waldo's brain. Then the figure, still in the daffodil hat and the fruited shoes, walked quickly to the bumpy edge of Waldo's brain and pressed the soft nakedness of the body against the frazzled gray hamburg of the brain. And it came alive.

"Yes," said Waldo.

"What is it then?" asked Dr. Wasserman.

"It's time to go," said Waldo.

And then the phone rang. Before Wasserman picked it up he said that he would take care of everything, Rugg, the whole business. Waldo, he said, was on his way.

Chapter Six

Ignoring his mother's scuffling above, Waldo polished his shoes in the cellar. He lit a cigarette when he was finished and stood before a peeling mirror.

There was not much that could be called professional about the man in the mirror. Mainly, he wasn't a man. It was, alas, still a boy that Waldo saw. And framing his face, beyond his brain, there were hobby horses, decayed ice skates, brittle albums and plain dry dust, residue and so forth that, if it *were* a man he was looking at, he would have burned or destroyed. But he had stored them, all these things which a boyish, if slightly scrambled, ego heaps upon itself.

Well, shit, thought Waldo, what should I expect? And standing among the dusty remains of a past which overlapped on an uncertain present, where walking did not mean moving, where screaming did not imply that someone was giving you a damn good licking, where bruises might be found only on those soft brain-ends, Waldo answered his own question: nothing.

Waldo tunneled through the mess of junk, shoving sleds this way and old clothes and stamp albums that way. And soon he was outside, back at the bus stop, without either his father or mother having seen his sneaky exit.

Waldo spent the first part of the bus ride dabbing lint from his sleeve and creasing his pants with his thumb and some saliva. A man next to him sighed.

Waldo turned.

The man said that he was going to run for President of the United States. "Why not?" the man asked. "I'm a citizen and I'm as good as any other sonofabitch in the country."

Before the bus stopped he had given Waldo a short whistle-stop-type speech. The man said that what the country needed was something to give it more spunk, more get-up-and-go. Like a war.

He asked Waldo if he would vote for him. Waldo promised he would.

*

Clovis was on time. She said she didn't like to wait.

"Where are the rest of the people?" asked Waldo touching at his tie.

"You drive. I'll ride and watch," said Clovis Techy flipping the bunch of keys to Waldo and vaulting the left protruding fin of her big Cadillac on her way to the front seat.

Waldo remarked about the seats being real leather. Clovis shrugged her lower lip. She said although it was made to *look* like leather it was better. No one would buy it if it didn't look like leather, she explained.

"I don't see anyone else here," Waldo repeated.

"I'm going to take you someplace you've never been," Clovis said.

"Didn't you say it's your birthday?"

"I think that's what I said."

"But there's no one here."

"You're here. I'm here. Aren't we somebody?"

"Yes," said Waldo.

"Who else do you want? If you want to be greedy I'll let you have your way," laughed Clovis.

Waldo thought a moment. He could think of no one he

would want along. He tried to think of someone, anyone, but all he could think of was the man in the bus that wanted to be President. Waldo couldn't remember what the man's face looked like.

"No one, I guess."

"When you come to the fork go left."

They rode on for some distance in caves shaped by the headlights. All around the car the darkness was thickening, and even inside the car it was dark. A small light under the dashboard did no more than make Clovis Techy's shoes look like a shiny clump of fresh fruit. Clovis did not speak. Waldo knew she was there, however, and was even glad that she was the only one who was. Waldo looked across once but could not distinguish Clovis's profile from the outside, now totally black.

"I have the feeling that we're going to get along very well," Clovis said. Waldo said nothing, continued driving.

"They keep this place secret," Clovis offered. "That way everyone makes sure they know about it. Everyone makes sure that they tell their friends about it. That's why they keep the place secret. Because it's good advertising."

"I see," said Waldo.

What Waldo saw finally was a gigantic white tower that looked very much like a peeled banana, pointing into the night sky, riddled now with the wide cones of searchlights. The tower stood erect, oblivious of the clusters of men and women gathering at its base, scurrying toward the red, round door of the tower. Each person flashed, rippled and contorted in the neon luminescence of a large sign above the door.

Clovis and Waldo got out of the car and walked toward the tower.

The large sign was impressive while Waldo approached, but up close it was just a spaghetti of black tubes. Waldo squinted at it as it gushed, pronged, and blinked, the black tangle of tubes animated to a Mazda minuet by some electrical genius located in the tower. While drippings of mercury leaped in the closed tubes and darted across the periphery of the tower one word stood out:

MANDRAKE

It remained bold, not blinking in the waterfall of lights. The persons entering shaded their eyes as they passed under it.

Streamers of mufti and chiffon fluttered inside the door. The walls had a bread-crumby texture, and inside the club proper there was a riot of bodies, pink-cheeked and drinking. Everything was fresh and clean and new. If there was a worm in this apple it was so far down, out of chawnking distance, that it didn't even matter.

Inside, a man said he was fed up to here. "Now, you take your ordinary buyer," he said. "He doesn't know ass from elbow about merchandising . . ." His voice trailed off as he shoved his way through the crowd. And Waldo and Clovis slowly made their own way through the asses and elbows.

"Watch out, honey," said a man pushing past Clovis. Then he said, "Here comes Rock Hudson." But it was the other Rock Hudson. This man was very short and his face looked like someone had been chewing it and had made a damned good meal out of it, too. He hurried up to a waitress but was out of breath when he finally reached her. He stood before her like a supper of cold leftovers and stank.

When the waitress and the man left the room, Clovis and Waldo took the man's empty table. The table seemed to be in the middle of the general confusion. Clovis said above the noise that she didn't think the man would be back for fifteen or twenty dollars at least. Waldo privately guessed correctly at the meaning of her oblique remark.

The table was behind a rubber fern. Waldo discovered it

was rubber, real rubber, only after he smelled it burning. A man a few feet away was wiping his cigar ashes on it absently as he pinched a rather old woman's neck vertebrae with his thumb and forefinger. Apparently, an attempt at eroticism.

The main room of the Mandrake Club was really a funnel decorated in what some interior decorators refer to as suburban Greco-Modern — simulated gold foil, plastic, fur, and Ionic ash trays. The funnel was divided into a series of concentric rings, each labeled with a glowing letter. Clovis and Waldo were in ring N, a respectable one. Ring A had sofas, M had cushions that were either sat upon or thrown. Ring E contained folding chairs and had access only to a fire exit. (The persons sitting in ring E were sullen.) In the center, at the hub of the rings, was a shallow pool surrounded by a narrow, doughnut-shaped dance floor. Couples yanked each other back and forth on the floor. In the pool were four logy ducks — large and golden-hued — bobbing among some plastic lotuses.

"See those ducks?" Clovis said. She pointed with the lighted end of her cigarette.

Waldo said he was looking at them.

"Take a good look," said Clovis. "Now, they look sick, don't they? But they're really not sick at all, or tired."

Waldo said he thought they looked down in the dumps.

Clovis agreed. "That," she said, "they are. But they're not sick. They're always like that. All ducks are. They look pooped but they're not, they look half-dead but they're not, they look everything but they're not. You see, each of those ducks is paddling like crazy underneath."

"They're not even moving," Waldo said.

"They're paddling like crazy underneath," Clovis repeated. "I know."

Waldo looked again at the ducks. They weren't moving.

But they were not close enough for Waldo to tell for sure. He looked around the Mandrake. It was a new neighborhood. There was no mistaking that. His old neighborhoods were mud puddles compared to the Mandrake Club. Even if, although he was not sure, the ducks were paddling like crazy underneath.

He watched the people eating. He thought how it made no difference who you were, you still ate the same if you were hungry. People were like that. You couldn't take food away from people. He remembered how his father would jam a chicken-bone in his mouth and talk through the bone as he trimmed the gristle. His mother chewing her corn flakes. Grammy gulping her milk, slurping it with her whole face, it seemed. Those six-minute meals, one minute of which was spent zipping the top off the Quikee Banquet ("Cook it in its Own Dish!") and popping it in and out of the oven.

"Asparagus," his father said.

"More?" his mother said.

"No," Grammy said.

"Drink your milk," his mother said.

"Remember how Gramps used to cry?" Grammy asked.

"Any dessert?" his father said.

"You want the world," his mother said.

"Egg in your beer, Edwin. That's what you always want," said Grammy.

"I break my butt for beans," his father said.

"Watch your language," his mother said.

Waldo looked back at the people in the Mandrake. The air was full of smoke and arms and red faces. Some people were merely panting at each other. One man's mouth hung open, as if his next movement would be to take a big bite of his wife, whose back was turned.

But the man did not bite her. Instead, he vomited, his

shoulders heaving back and forth. His wife turned to him. She asked him if he had called her. Then she saw what he had done and turned back to her friends. One of the persons she was with said he thought that was the funniest thing she had said all evening. Soon the woman too was laughing.

Other men snapped shut the lids of their heavy chromium-plated cigarette lighters. When they inhaled the smoke their faces registered pain, but the look of pain was replaced by one of relief when they exhaled.

Clovis watched and listened intently. When Waldo looked at her he saw people dancing on her large eyes. Lights flashed, too, so Waldo faced Clovis instead of watching the people. Voices rapped against Waldo's ears. Somebody called somebody else a perfect dog. Then on the main entrance to Clovis's eye an old man appeared. He doddered in. The man paused for breath and took his cigar out of his mouth as he gazed down at the funnel filled with laughter, the smoke hanging in ropy clouds.

Clovis looked up at the man and then she said to Waldo, "That's old Jasper Pistareen."

"Old Jasper. Sure."

The tinkling of a piano started. Then it was joined by the steady repetition of a thud-thud, as if someone were beating on a hollow log. These two separate sounds were accompanied after a while by the long insistent howling of a eunuch voice. The voice said give me love, love, love. That's all I want.

A man in a dark suit at the next table produced a newspaper and started reading to a group of disinterested persons. "Listen to this. It'll crack you up. *He started laughing when a friend's balloon exploded. He kept on laughing for several minutes until he fainted. Doctors could not revive him.* Isn't that the greatest!" Then the man laughed, kept on laughing, but he did not faint.

The wife said, "He gets stiff and thinks he's Rock Hudson. Pretty soon he'll start honking again."

The old woman near the rubber fern: "I think you're pretty swell, too. How about another whuchamacallit."

The elderly man, Jasper, was swaying, threatening to fall forward. A girl in tinsel, seeing the man's vertigo, grabbed him expertly at her hip. With some aplomb she half escorted, half dragged the quavering Jasper below. He waved to people as he descended to ring M, near the ducks.

A little man showed some snapshots to the group of people that sat around the man with the newspaper. For laughs, he said, no one gets hurt. The man with the newspaper continued to read and titter. He ignored the man with the snapshots. "And there were signs of sexual assault. With a blunt instrument," he said. The snapshots were passed around. The men kept on reading.

"Clovis?" Waldo saw that Clovis looked at the people with a sweet smile.

A man with a huge badge that said MY NAME IS BUSTER. WHAT'S YOURS? leaned over to another man at the same table and said confidentially, "I'm in wingnuts. You?" But he was interrupting a conversation about death and how one woman really got it in the ear when her late mother died, her own mother, from something or other, no one knew for sure. Buster could not help overhearing, he said, and told about his own mother, bless her soul, who at that very minute not only was completely wormproof but had a bunch of daisies, fresh ones, at her feet. By the time he stopped talking the conversation had turned to breakfasts and the woman who had gotten it all in the ear told about her very special diet. "It's full-bodied," she said, "already chewed and flavored. It has, I don't know, tang."

"Clovis?"

Buster, seeing that the table was a dead loss, tapped a perfect stranger on the shoulder and said, "See that babe with the big jugs? Well, when the Moose met last year in Bayonne . . ."

"Clovis?"

She stirred.

"Clovis!" Waldo shouted. "Mrs. Techy!"

Clovis blinked out the activity in the Mandrake. "What?" She looked at Waldo.

"Happy birthday."

"Same to you," came the cranky answer. She seemed to be returning a swear. Waldo apologized. "Don't say you're sorry. It's my birthday, you wished me a happy birthday. That's natural. I'm aging. I take what I get — every single goddamned happy birthday. So don't be sorry." Clovis sipped her drink and then added, "Anyway, a lot of good being sorry does."

Waldo decided to change the subject. He mentioned Wasserman.

"He's a sick bastard," said Clovis.

"He's okay," said Waldo. "He's not so bad."

"I didn't say he wasn't okay and I didn't say," Clovis belched, "he was bad. What I said was *he's a sick bastard!*" Clovis was getting drunk and the words were coming out in lumps. "What kind of an eye doctor is it that doesn't wear glasses? You tell me."

"*Does* he wear glasses?"

"I forget," said Clovis.

"Guess I never took a good look," said Waldo trying to think if Wasserman did or didn't wear glasses.

"Let's suppose he does," Clovis went on. "What did he ever tell you that mattered one way or the other?"

"He used to talk to me while he was testing my eyes. He said that I should admit that I hated my father and loved my mother. I said I hated them both and he said that was impossible. It was against the rules, he said. What rules? I said, I just hate them, that's all. It's against the rules of psychoanalysis, he said."

"Psychoanalysis," said Clovis, "it's really giving sex a bad name."

"You think so?" asked Waldo. "I always thought sex had a bad press."

"That too," said Clovis. "But what can we do about it? It's a losing battle."

"I think I can do something about it," said Waldo. "I was thinking about what Wasserman said about college, about how I could find myself there. I said I'd think about it, and I have been thinking about it, about leaving home and finding myself. Maybe be a reporter with one of those hats and know everyone in town, do good, travel around, learn to type on a typewriter and like that. After a while I'll be able to give sex — and a lot of other things — a good name. The only trouble is I don't know much about newspapers and I've never been . . . well . . . "

"You can be frank with me," said Clovis.

"Laid," said Waldo.

"Which college did Wasserman mention?" asked Clovis.

"Rugg," said Waldo.

"I just want you to understand one thing. It's a common misconception among the youth of today that you have to go to college to lose your virginity. That's all wrong. You can lose it just as easily in the back seat of a car, if you can afford the car, or in a movie for the small price of a seat in the balcony. It saves wear and tear. God knows, I lost mine in a choir loft halfway through a hymn."

"I think I need a change of scenery. And I'd like to be a writer or a reporter," Waldo said. He thought of himself as a reporter: it was the same as being a spy only you didn't get killed. Not only did you get paid, but you also got your name in the paper every day.

"At your age — you're a growing boy — you shouldn't be cooped up," Clovis said. "Or at any age." Clovis frowned and looked straight ahead. She said very loudly that she liked Waldo quite a bit and thought he should get out, go away.

"I'd like to clear out," said Waldo.

"But," said Clovis, "you don't want to flap so far that you can't get back. Just go someplace where it doesn't hurt." She didn't say what. She mentioned something about life being too short. She handed Waldo a box. Waldo opened it. Inside the box was an odd-looking device with a strap. "A present," said Clovis.

"Is it a watch?" asked Waldo.

"You've got to keep track somehow," said Clovis. "It tells the time of the day, the day of the week, the month and the year. That little blue thing on the side turns pink when it's going to rain."

"Jesus Christ," said Waldo.

"The only thing it doesn't do is tell your fortune. But who wants to know *that!*" Clovis said that she had one. She couldn't live without it, although she carried it in her purse. It looked pushy if you had it on your wrist all the time. Clovis said that time was very important. What was the use in going through all the hello-how-are-you-you-old-son-of-a-bitch stuff? And all the conversations that began, say-you-come-from-such-and-such? Do-you-know-so-and-so-who-used-to-rape-girls? And all that. You could save time if you got right down to business, to brass tacks.

"Yes," said Waldo.

"So, when do you want to sleep with me?" Clovis Techy asked, getting right down to business.

"You mean *sleep?*"

"I mean *sleep*," said Clovis, getting down to brass tacks. Waldo shrugged because Clovis would not have understood a twitch. And then he said, "When?"

"When," said Clovis. "You'll notice I didn't say why or where."

"I noticed," said Waldo. But that was all he said for a long moment. Then he got an inspiration. When he saw Clovis put a cigarette in her mouth he thought of a movie he had once seen. Waldo fumbled in his pocket for a match and then, leaning way over and looking past the match to Clovis, he lit her cigarette. That, according to what Waldo figured popular opinion, was as close to lust as you could get in a restaurant. At this point Waldo twitched, but luckily the twitch surfaced as a wink.

Clovis winked back. "I've been reading about colleges," she said. "You might even like it at . . . what was that name again?"

"Rugg."

"Yes, Rugg," said Clovis. "I think you might like it there. Of course, I don't trust these magazine articles one single bit. I'd like to get the real inside story from you."

"I used to be editor of the newspaper at Booneville."

"Sure you did," said Clovis.

"I could report everything to you."

"Sure you could," said Clovis. She looked up and saw the man called Jasper Pistareen starting up the stairs toward them. Clovis called to him.

The old man called Jasper Pistareen walked over. Clovis introduced him to Waldo. Waldo said he was glad to meet him.

"Likewise," said the man.

"He's going to college," said Clovis.

"You don't say," said Jasper.

"I guess I am," said Waldo.

"What for? I mean, what for are you going?"

"What kind of a question is that?" Clovis asked.

"Just a question question. No offense intended." Jasper laughed.

"What are you in now?" Clovis asked Jasper.

"News. Well," Jasper backed off a bit, "not *real* news. But sweaty stories about how I was raped ninedy times or how I gave birth to a calf-shaped fag. Lotsa pictures and lotsa twisted classifieds like boy with saddle would like to meet same with whip. Or the couple bit. Couple in their twennies would like to meet same with modern ideas on nudism and weekends. They're all nuts but it's a living. They gotta live."

"And so do you," said Clovis.

"And so do I," said Jasper. "It's a living. I figure in a few months we'll be breaking into the real news bit, scoops and crap like that. But there's no demand right now. I can make my bundle in sweaty stories."

"What do you make of this guy?" Clovis said jokingly to Waldo.

"It all sounds very whadyoucallit interesting," said Waldo. That's what he said. But what he was thinking was: *I'd like to meet a nice simple little girl.*

"If you ever get sick of college drop around the office. I can use someone like you," said Jasper.

Waldo looked at the man. "I used to be on the newspaper at Booneville."

"The Booneville *pen?* You were in the pen?" Jasper's face crinkled with pleasure.

"Yeah," Waldo said trying to imitate Otto Noon for the moment and forgetting that his only crime was burning his father's truss and pouring motor oil in the hopper and molasses in the penny bank.

"I was in the pen when I was about your age. Pretty raunchy, eh?"

The two convicts shared their joke. "Yeah," said Waldo, "pretty raunchy."

"Sometimes I get to thinking it really wasn't so bad," said Jasper. "I mean, if you can take all the raunch. Lotta crap in the pen. Lotta laughs too."

"A few laughs," said Waldo.

"A *few!* Man, I was laughing the whole time. I was in with a bunch of great guys." Jasper paused and shook his head recalling the bunches of great guys. "Them were the days. I was in with some funny guys — real funny senses of humor, you know. Like this one time . . ." he began. But Clovis interrupted him.

"Look, Jasper, we'll look you up. We got some things to talk about."

Jasper winked. "Sure, you do that. And . . . ah . . . fella. If you ever wanna job you look me up. We'll talk over old times." Then he went up to Waldo, grinned, and punched Waldo in the stomach. "Ya still a kid, too, ya sonofabitch! Hahahahahahaha."

"Hahahaha," Waldo said. His stomach hurt, although the punch was meant good naturedly.

Jasper saw a friend of his across the room. He shouted and then was gone.

"You'll like college," said Clovis.

"I didn't know it was definite."

"You want to go?" Clovis raised her eyebrows to prove that it was a question. "You go right ahead and go."

"But the money . . ."

Clovis snatched Waldo's hand. She looked fierce, as if she was going to stab him with her nose. "Wait a minute. Wait a minute. Now let's get one thing straight — I don't want

to hear you utter that word once more. You can't afford to."
She bit off each word. "You let me say it. You got that
straight?"

"Okay."

"Watch it," said Clovis. Her face still looked angry. But
in the silence the music from the Mandrake Stage drifted up.
A man was singing a song about the whole world being a
candy store.

"Which reminds me," said Clovis. "But when I was a little
girl I had a friend who saved his pennies for a whole year.
When he got about two hundred he went into a candy store
and bought about fifty kinds of candy and ate it all the same
day."

"And then he died," said Waldo conclusively.

"Ah-hah!" shouted Clovis. "No he didn't! He didn't die
from the *candy*, that is. But he got sick and when they tried
to pump out his stomach he strangled on the rubber tube
they stuck in his throat and *then* he died."

"It's the same thing, isn't it?"

"Technically no," said Clovis. She repeated it.

"Okay," said Waldo.

"Anyway, the important thing is what do you want to do?"

"Do?"

"Be. What do you want to be?"

"You mean *job?*"

"I mean *be*. What do you want to be, who do you want to
be, where do you want to be?"

Waldo thought a moment. "I . . . dunno. I got a charge
out of writing the newspaper at Booneville."

"You got a charge out of writing a newspaper at Booneville. If it gives you a charge you should be it. What do you
call someone that writes a newspaper? A journalist? A reporter?"

"A reporter. That's what I want to be, a reporter."

"You go to college and learn how. College should be pretty ducky. You be a good boy and go. I hope you won't let me down," said Clovis. "I am placing my trust in you," she said patting Waldo on his left knee.

Waldo felt something come apart when she did it. It was a ripping or tearing sensation, like the crackling sound of a television set being snapped on, a humming as the picture flipped into focus. He liked it. She did it again on his other leg. Waldo was transported.

Just before they left the Mandrake Waldo glanced back. He saw the people sliding around the dance floor and was reminded of those dung-colored lizards that can look like orchids whenever they feel like it. From a distance everything looked peachy. Even the ducks in the pool bobbing up and down among the plastic lotuses. Even they could have been happy.

*

Clovis had not spoken. Waldo had climbed into the driver's seat and now they were speeding back over the road that led away from the Mandrake. The lights of the club flashed in the rear view mirror and distracted Waldo for a while, and then they were lost.

Clovis's first words were an emotionless request to turn down a side road. The words came out of the darkness next to Waldo. He obeyed. The car jounced on the bumps and then fell into the ruts and humped up the steep grades. When they could go no farther (they were at the edge of a big lake) Clovis told Waldo to shut off the engine.

The lights went out. They sat in the darkness for almost a full minute until Waldo heard the leather seat exhaling slowly. He smelled the perfume of Clovis; it got stronger and stronger until it was all around him and made his skin shrink. When he looked beside him, just barely making out the vague shape of the woman's face, he heard the whisper. It was soft, not anxious or urgent, with careful emphasis. It did prevent Waldo from hearing his watch tick.

"Now you give me a present."

Waldo slid from the steering wheel and put his arm around Clovis and looked at the water and listened to the glug-glug of either the water or some frogs in it. He felt absurd sitting there, his arm around a grown woman. So he kissed her cheek. Her cheek was not hot, scorching; it felt like rubber. Clovis did nothing. He kissed her on the mouth. When he did that Clovis flicked her tongue into his mouth, and Waldo moved his hand across her left breast.

"That's a breast," said Clovis.

Waldo flicked his tongue into her mouth. Clovis put her hand on Waldo's leg. And so forth. It was like two swimmers slapping each other to get up the circulation just before they plunged in; hand on breast, stomach, leg, tongues lunging; it may not have been what some people call passion but it did the trick.

Clovis finally pushed Waldo away. While Waldo apologized Clovis held the neckline of her dress and fumbled. When she found what she was looking for she gave a hard pull. A zipper, the length of the entire dress, opened and exposed the real Clovis. That was all there was to it. She shook off her dress and then dived into the back seat.

She did not have to wave to Waldo to join her. Not exactly in a flash, but very soon Waldo was on her, a swimmer negotiating his way, paddling, urging forward, trying to stay on course, then in long strokes, glug-glugging along in the darkness, a swimmer learning the strokes and being cheered by the water itself. It hurt, Waldo decided, but still he paddled toward a tiny flame.

Chapter Seven

"Where?" His mother turned completely around in her chair and dropped a book of little stamps in her lap. Two small green stamps adhered to her tongue, thrust out in disgust. She asked Waldo to repeat the word.

"College," said Waldo.

"*What?!*" his father yelled angrily. He straightened up after pausing for a moment to adjust the knobs on the television set. He faced his son. Behind him the television blew noise into the room. The music was pounding along with a fear-stricken man charging around a mountain at a great rate.

"Haven't got time to explain. I'm leaving."

"You just got back from being away —"

"I was in the pen."

"*Again!*" wailed his mother. "You want to leave *again*."

"I've got a few things to say to you, boy," his father said. "Waldoooo!"

But Waldo had gone.

Waldo's father looked for the suitcase, but it was nowhere to be seen. He dropped into his beach chair of aluminum tubes and canvas webbing and put his arms on both armrests. In his undershirt and shower clogs he slightly resembled Abraham Lincoln seated wisely and immovably in the Lincoln Memorial. The one people take pictures of. He sat still, his head tilted forward toward the tube. His wife contemplated the book of stamps with her good eye, then picked up the book and slowly pasted the remaining ones onto a new page. The licking noises bothered Waldo's father and he had to turn up the volume of the running man on the television several times before his wife completed her page.

Part Two

Chapter Eight

Waldo had already decided that what he really wanted to do was meet a nice simple girl, fairly well upholstered and fairly jolly.

His pockets bulged with money. It squirted from between his fingers. Waldo did not bother to count it. Clovis had promised him as much as he wanted. It was a present. If Waldo had counted the money it would have implied a certain price on his head. So he didn't count his money and still it squirted out.

Waldo was thinking of the nice simple girl as he rode to Rugg on the bus. The bus was hot and the dry air was filled with spores and pollen. The bus rocked and Waldo responded sluggishly, his feet on the seat in front, knees against his chest. His head bobbed forward every time the driver tapped the brake. Only slightly did Waldo hear the wheezing of the engine, and once the bus got beyond the numbered streets, the stoplights at each corner, the large buildings, the people running at the cars, wild-eyed, dragging dogs on leashes, the wheezing stopped and the only sound was a steady humming from the sinuses of the engine over which Waldo was curled.

Waldo stirred occasionally from his sleep. He would raise his head and squint momentarily at his knee, out the window, into the aisle, then his head would drop and be caught by his limp neck.

His eyes were closed tightly. Waldo saw nothing until,

among the marbles and streaks, a man came walking. The man took a pistol out of his pocket and walked along the streaky avenue, visible only as he passed under the street lights. He stopped in front of a house, flipped his cigarette away, checked his pistol, and entered. Inside he slipped into bed with a woman.

Waldo woke up perspiring. He looked out the window when he felt the bus slowing down. He tried to clean the dirt off the window, but after rubbing it a moment he realized that all the dirt was on the outside.

The bus came to a halt and several people got on. At the head of the line was a slim blond girl. She had risen up the steps, out of the dust of the little town, and she looked down the aisle before she began walking. Suddenly she leaped in the air and took a great breath; her arms shot out and she fell into the lap of a man sitting next to the aisle. She had crushed the man's newspaper. The man struggled with his newspaper, finally got it out from under the girl intact, and turned it inside out in order to read the comics flat.

There was a boy behind her, a tall stupid-looking boy with a duffel bag and a delicious nose. The boy fixed his glasses tightly on the bridge of his nose and walked to the back of the bus. The lenses of the glasses were like large hailstones. They obscured the boy's eyes with nacre an inch thick. As the boy passed the girl (still in the man's lap) he laughed; the people around hissed their sympathies to the girl. The boy threw his duffel bag over Waldo's head to the luggage rack above and sat heavily next to Waldo. He said immediately, "Can't even goose a broad any more without everyone bitching. A real buncha candy-asses. Wanna cigarette?"

Then the boy went to sleep.

An hour later the bus was still moving. Waldo tried not to sleep. He was afraid the man with the pistol would still be scouting around. Waldo looked at the boy next to him. The

boy was still sleeping, his arms folded across his chest. Looking sideways at the boy, Waldo saw the boy's eyes. They
were little things, slits, crusted shut. The boy's head jitter-
bugged — the road was very bumpy.

"I goosed her," he said, his eyes still closed. "And everyone
got mad. Did you get mad?"

"No," said Waldo quickly. And then he thought of the
girl. She was a nice simple girl. "But you shouldn't have
done that."

The boy's eyes were still closed. "Three A.M. in the morning," he began. "We were near this park watching this lady
hitting a guy with her pocketbook. We were just standing
there spitting on the sidewalk — a bunch of us, no one knew
anyone else, except we were all interested in this crazy broad
hitting the guy. About five of us. So the lady was really
knocking the shit out of the guy and screaming, look what
you've made me do, you sonofabitch, I hate you. Then naturally she got tired of hitting the guy and she dropped the
pocketbook and they hugged each other and kissed and she
cried. So while this was all going on the guy next to me starts
laughing and then he turns to me and says he thinks it's pretty
funny, stupid-funny, he says. I agreed. And then he says he
knows I'm a Jew because only a Jew could watch the whole
thing and understand. And so is he a Jew. Except he looks
like an A-rab. He lisps a little so I say to myself the guy's a
fag, too. The bastard was everything. But I was sure he was
a fag because he says after a while, although his aunt lives
with him there's still a lot of privacy in his apartment and
why don't I come up and visit him? I gave him my address
and walked away. About a week later I get a postcard from
him. How was I?"

"Just like that?" said Waldo wondering what happened to
the lady who assaulted her husband and then cried.

"Just like that I met Fred Wolfpits."

"I see," said Waldo.

"You do?"

"What's your name?" Waldo asked, almost timidly.

"What's yours?"

"Waldo."

"What kinda name is that?"

"It's my name. Do you go to Rugg?"

"Do you?"

"I guess so."

"You *guess* so? If you don't you're on the wrong bus."

"I'm just starting."

"You're just *star*ting?"

"Yes, just starting."

"What're you starting?"

"Journalism. I want to be a . . ."

"*Journal*ism? You mean newspapers?"

"Stuff like that."

"You shoulda taken abnormal."

"Abnormal what?"

"Psych. Ab psych."

"I know a psychologist. I don't want to be one."

"That's all newspapers print . . ."

"I don't think he's an abnormal psychologist."

". . . case histories."

"So why are you going to Rugg?"

"To see Fred Wolfpits," said the boy. And that was all he said until the bus arrived in Amnion.

Amnion was the last stop on the bus line. It was the home of Rugg College and many laundromats. When the bus stopped the boy with the glasses turned to Waldo and said, "Morris Porter."

Waldo started to get up, but Morris Porter was blocking the aisle and did not move. Morris stared through his big lenses and pointed to the window spotted with dirt. "Look at all those crazy bastards." Then he laughed. He had a laugh that leaped in his skinny neck, hooked itself on his Adam's apple, bobbled that, then unhooked and flew out of his mouth. Each laugh was a separate distinct *ha*.

Morris picked up his duffel bag and walked off the bus. They were the last to leave. Waldo looked for the nice simple girl but she had gone.

"Let's go see what's up," said Morris, and he led the way across the street to a multicolored bar with the sign CHA-MELEON painted on a large board over the door.

"Party," said someone to Morris as he entered. The place was full of students. Waldo noticed they had a worrisome sameness about them; their clothes, their glassless eyes, their faces ruddy and noseless. Waldo was surprised at how healthy they looked, stuffed with food and muscle.

"Party," a boy near Morris said, but this time it was not said to Morris. Morris turned to Waldo when they were at the center of the milling students. He cupped his hand to his mouth: "They *look* harmless, but when you consider that every person is lugging around about eighteen unhappy glands, then you realize you got something to worry about."

In the center of the room a boy with a guitar sang:

> *Wheraiver min are fahtin fer thar rahts*
> *Thass where Ahm gonna beeeee!*

The circle of students around the singer held hands. Each wore a look of protest as if, right then and there, in the Chameleon, they would establish law and order, and if not beauty, justice.

"That's where the folksingers sit," said Morris. "The foreign students and most of the Jews sit right near there. The Negro sits in that chair, when he comes. The football players at the other end. The grad students near the Jews and folk-singers. The profs near the shithouse so no one can see them when they take a leak. The fags have their own table, so do the Republicans, though some of the Democrats are between the Jews and the folksingers and some are near the profs. The fat kids that aren't football players are near the coke machine. Fred Wolfpits sits over there . . ."

"Fred . . ."

"I told you about him. He lives in the cellar of my rooming house . . . By the way, where are *you* living?"

"I don't know. I figured I'd look around."

"Why look around? There's room in the Watershed."

"The Watershed?"

"I call it the Watershed because the guy that runs it is a jerk named Watershed. Gull Watershed. It's a rooming house. I got the whole attic for myself. Fred lives in the cellar."

"Okay," said Waldo.

"Let's go over right now. We can dump our stuff, then I'll show you the other places around here."

As they were leaving a boy came up to Morris and began talking very rapidly and laughing. "Party," was all that Waldo heard. The boy said it several more times.

Soon, Waldo and Morris stood before the large brown house which Morris called the Watershed. On the lawn of the house were little animals — not real ones, but plastic flamingoes and celluloid teddy bears.

Waldo followed Morris up the stairs, left his suitcase in the room, looked out the window at the lawn, then, when he found out the name of Gull Watershed's wife, asked Morris if there was a phone in the building.

"Gull and Dove Watershed," Waldo said into the phone. Clovis said he had all the luck; she would send him some money right off.

Waldo went outside. Morris was on the other side of the
street talking to a blond girl. A nice simple girl. It was the
girl Morris had goosed on the bus. When Waldo walked
over to meet her, she turned and went away.

*

Morris pointed through the fog that hung like thick anes-
thetic draperies over the buildings of Rugg College. "Take a
good look," he said. He thought a moment, then said, "You
know the guy I was talking to at the Chameleon?"
Waldo nodded.
"Well, he was telling me about this party."
"Which party?"
"This party here that we're going to have. Anyway . . . I
forget what I was going to say."
Waldo was going to ask more about the party, but he
thought that if the party was so important he would hear
about it sooner or later. He looked across the artificial pond
with Morris. On the other side Rugg lay silent before them.
Morris said that Rugg and Amnion overlapped. They were
isolated from any other town by the mountains which rose
above them on every side. The mountains seemed to prevent
the fog from leaving the Amnion Valley. This isolation, as
well as Rugg's architecture, caused Rugg to resemble a motel
that might be found on the desert outside a large city, on a
side road. Rugg was new, but even though it was a college it
had a lot in common with the Booneville School for Delinquent Boys: large panes of glass, reinforced concrete and
aluminum and flat graveled roofs. Rugg was composed of
many one-story buildings and had ramps instead of stairs.
Boreal Hall (the Treasurer's Office, the IBM machines, the
complex of punched cards and secretaries) was at the center.
The parking lot and the heat and power plant were to the
left rear of Boreal Hall. At greater distances were the Presi-

dent's House, the cage (a physical education building which Morris said was "the largest cage in the country" according to the Official Catalogue), the classrooms and the library. In the darkness outside the campus were the professors' homes, the freshman dorms and rooming houses which had to be provided since there was not enough dormitory space available.

A long elm-shaded road led up to the flattened rectangle which was Boreal Hall. This structure, because it was at the very top of Campus Hill, dominated, and could be seen from quite a distance.

Waldo squinted through the fog, but he was not looking at anything in particular. "Who was that girl you were talking to, Morris?"

"The girl I was talking to. *Which* girl?"

"The blonde. The one you goosed on the bus."

Morris thought. "Mona?"

"Mona?"

"Mona."

Chapter Nine

"I'm talking to *you* out there. Welcome to Rugg! Arnold Wermy's the name, but you'll be calling me Duff soon's I get to know each and every one of you. My story starts long before any of you were born. About the Second Ice Age, hahahahaha. When Rugg and I were jest little fellas I got to figuring. I said to myself, Duff, if you don't get off your butt and get a college education you're gonna be in a peck of trouble, cause all those guys you see hitting the books left and right are gonna be way the deuce ahead of you. But I knew more than them. I was a big shot and hard to convince — I was a pigheaded sonofagun, you know what I mean? So darn-it-all if I didn't go into the army and I was stabbing my bayonet into a sandbag one day and I got to figuring again. But it was no use because I was signed up. Well, to make a long story short, I knocked around a bit and I went into the beer joints with all the guys — a buncha swell guys. But, not too much up here, if you know what I mean. Well, the CO shot about a dozen platoons down to Texas. I'll never forget that town — Happy, Texas, with a swell little church. Well, my buddy comes up to me one day and says to me, Duff, he says, you waste a heckofallotta time, if you know what I mean. And I knew what he meant. I knew, I'm ashamed to say. And I said to myself back there in Happy, Texas: Duff, when you get your papers and you're done with Uncle Sam and you get yourself back to Amnion and the rest, you jest sign up for a hitch at Rugg College. In other words, wise up, I said. And darned if I didn't do it and here I am talking to all you swell guys and gals out there who did it, too, just like I did it back there in the Second Ice Age. Hahahahaha. And you all got your reasons. You're darn tootin' you got your reasons — don't let anyone tell you any different. You stick to your guns and you'll be okay. I did. Old Duff knows and old Duff cares and don't let anyone tell you any different. Thing is, Rugg can take you to water, but it can't make you drink unless you're thirsty for knowledge. Gotta have that thirst. A few things I picked up along the way. And glad to pass them along, guys and gals. Never forget, a book in the hand is worth ten in the library. Education is like a good cigar — you gotta smoke every bit of it to get the most out of it. Even if it makes you sick. Especially. Life's funny that way. You gotta learn to work. All young people do. I'm not talking about studying really. I mean, get out and dig a hole some day — get your hands dirty, get all tuckered out, kill yourself working out in God's fresh air. Buckle right down and tackle the thing. Take off your clothes — *coat*, I mean, hahaha, and roll up them sleeves and jump right in, no fooling. Now I know what each and every one of you is saying to yourself right now . . ."

*

"I said, *good*."
"Sure."
"He was always a good boy, Edwin, and you know it."
"Watch out for the pins."
"You're not listening to a word."
"Yes, I am."
"No, you're not."
"Do you think that next time, Emma, it would be possible for you to buy fish without pins? You know, I . . ."

"Just that nasty business at home."

"*Another* one!"

"The dirty stuff with your truss and then the toilet business."

"The *what?*"

"The toilet business."

"*Which* toilet business? Or should I say *whose?*"

". . . if he thinks he can make a fool out of me he's got another thing coming."

"You mean with the oil?"

"Books, most likely. I've got to hand it to Walter. He made the best of *jail.*"

"Don't say that word, Emma. Say, there's another pin. Just put it beside my plate and take another piece like this if you don't mind."

"I don't . . ."

"Good. Cause my tongue was hanging out . . ."

". . . care about us really. We'll soon enough be dead . . ."

"Don't say that word, Emma. I don't like it one bit."

" . . and you know it, Edwin. I'm only looking after his own good, you know. God knows, we *have* done our best to raise him proper. Why, I don't remember one time that he has ever spoken to me. I mean, *really* spoken to me or asked advice or said, 'Gee, Mom, you're sure dressed terrific,' or 'Gosh, Mom, this sure is a swell meal.' Other mothers get it. I never got it. I never once remember . . ."

"Emma?"

"Yes?"

"You like fish, don't you?"

"Yes, I do. I guess I've . . ."

"And you know that I'm just wild about fresh fish?"

"Fresh fish. Yes, Edwin, I always think of you. I always think of you. I love you, Edwin. Have you forgotten so . . ."

"No, I'm not complaining again about your bad cooking or your infernal gabbing . . ."

"No, Edwin, certainly you're not."

". . . but do you think that it would be humanly possible . . ."

"You just have to ask, Edwin. You just have to say the wor . . ."

". . . to buy fish without pins in it. My mouth is a running sore from those goddamned things! Look, I'm *bleeding*."

"Oh, my poor Edwin is all *bleedy!*"

"It hurts like blue blazes."

"Like blue blazes! Well, let me do something."

"Don't get up, Emma. It's too late. Pass me the paper, will you?"

"Too late. I *am* sorry, Edwin. Those horrible pins. Why did they ever put them in there anyway? It's more than I can understand."

"Why did who put what in there?"

"The pins. In the fish. Fish-pins. Why did they put them in there so we could get all bleeding?"

"*God* put them in there. They're *born* with them, for God's sake. It's forgotten. It doesn't hurt no more. Now, will you forget it!"

"Don't yell. I don't care what you do. But don't yell."

"I'm not yelling!"

"You are yelling, Edwin. You just yelled."

"Mmm. Hey, Emma?"

"Yes."

"What's the name of the — I think it's a quiz show — that you choose your questions by breaking balloons by dancing on the balloons, and then you have to answer . . ."

"How should I know? You're the TV expert around here."

"What was that?"

"I said, *you're the TV expert around here!*"

"No, the other thing. It sounded like . . ."

"Well, I can't hear myself think, so I don't know how . . ."

"For your information, Emma, I *can* hear myself think."

"It's the phone."

"So it's the phone."

"You asked. I didn't."

"I don't care any more."

"*Answer* it!"

"Answer it yourself."

"You're a *meanie*. That's all you are, Edwin."

"Okay, I'm a meanie. At least I'm not a shit-head like you."

"You're a garbage-mouth and you know it."

"Hello? Yes. Um. Um. Uh-huh. Yuh. Wouldn't be a bit surprised . . ."

"Who is it?"

"It's . . . wait a sec . . . the cemetery. It's Oak Grove. Wait a minute . . . um . . . yuh . . . trying to talk to three people at once. Sorry, hahaha. Sure, go right ahead. Like I said, I wouldn't be . . ."

*

". . . working the daylights out of them, you know what I mean? But all work and no play makes Jack a dull boy. Or Jill, hahaha. Swell, kids, just swell. What I'm trying to drive home is that and nothing more. Just remember Duff Wermy's story about the hill of red ants whenever you get a test. That's what I used to do — and look where it got *me!* Hahaha. But. In closing. Let me thank each and every one of you out there — cause I'm talking to you and you and you — for coming. And remember, don't think of me as your president, although that's exactly what I am and it took a heck of a lot of work and initiative to get me where I am today talking to each and every one of you down there. No, think of me as your buddy, your big brother away from house and home. Sure it's tough to be away from home. You're all leaving houses and girlfriends with heaps of living in them. Your mom and dad worked hard to send you here to get some book learning — they love you like all get-out. Sure, no one likes to leave mom and her familiar old apron and her pies and cakes. I used to see guys — grown men — crying their eyes out down there in Texas, beating their sad old heads on the barracks floor just so's they could get furlough time to see their best girl. You probably never seen grown men crying like babies. I have. And I can tell you it's not a pretty sight. But there's a reason, and a darned good reason it is, for going away from home to make something of yourself. You simply got to work and sacrifice and go away from home. The communists are over there working like mad. Sure they wish they were here. They don't like wearing those stupid clothes. They're very unhappy people. Never a smile. That's cause they're sick and tired of being communists and they want a few things for themselves like we have. But we gotta work and sacrifice because they're trying very, very hard to kill each and every one of you out there. They're dying to get here and take over. *And we're not going to let them!* I swear, if we don't do our level best you're going to have to learn to speak Russian. And it's a damn hard language to learn. It's a wonder how they do it. They got jails there for people that don't shape up. Do we have jails here if you don't shape up? Not a one! And if I hear any of you saying we do you're going to find yourself in a bind! Anyway, work together, have a dream, live and learn. If you got a beef with the administration take it down to the office and we'll chew the fat. We're all here to help you become good citizens and smart voters. You be square with us, we'll be square with you. And don't forget . . . call me Duff or I'll break your neck. Hahahahahahahahaha—"

Chapter Ten

The bell of Morris's heart-shaped alarm clock rang against Waldo's ear. He shifted in bed and tried to block out the sounds, but the sounds persisted giggling against his head. Waldo reached for the clock. It was gone, yet the sound was louder than ever. Waldo groaned when he opened his eyes and saw what hovered above him.

His father, frowning, stood over him, his arms outstretched as if he were presenting a gift. In his left hand the alarm clock vibrated. He held it at arm's length to Waldo's ear. He seemed to be imitating one of those useless gadgets that are sometimes found in gift shops.

Waldo, having just been shaken out of the soft branches of sleep, was confused by what he saw. In back of the man with the clock was a woman, attached to the man somehow, her head tilted slightly to the side. She looked as if she were about to bob forward to forecast rain. But the tableau did not shift. The stumpy man with the clock remained grim. And still the alarm sounded.

"Do you know what time it is, son?" asked the man with the clock.

"What the hell . . ." Waldo started.

The woman spoke. "You remember us? That's your father there with the clock. I'm your . . ."

"I know who you are! But did you have to wake me up like this? I mean, for godsakes . . ."

"Will you listen to him, Edwin? Using that language . . ."

"WILL YOU SHUT OFF THAT ALARM CLOCK RIGHT NO . . ."

Miraculously the clock ran down. Waldo's father bent over slowly and put the clock on Waldo's stomach. Then he shook his head saying, "I would've let it run all day. I'm telling you, I would've let that clock . . ."

"I don't think he knows who we are, Edwin."

"You're right, you know that? You're right. Why, I said to myself . . ."

"Okay, okay." Irritation was giving way to inflammation and eruption. Waldo was talking fast. "Now I'd just like to know what you mean by coming in here and setting the alarm clock back and letting it ring until I lose both my eardrums! I'd just like to know who gives you the right to wake me out of a sound sleep! I'd just like to know . . ."

"He'd just like to know! *Who* do you think you're talking to, young man? Just who do you think you're talking to?"

"YOU! *That's who!*" Waldo was screaming. "YOU — both of you!"

"Why you . . ." The woman came forward clumsily. She banged against the bedpost at the height of her fury.

The man steadied her. "Take it easy, Emma. He doesn't know what he's saying."

"Like hell I don't know what I'm saying!" Waldo got out of bed. He was hopping into his pants, unable to think of anything further to say, as he said, "I know what I'm saying . . . I know what I'm saying . . ."

"Why, going off like that. You think a sane person would go off like that? You think a sane person would do what he's done? A sane person wouldn't . . ."

"I'm a sane person! I came here mainly to get away from the whole herd of you, to learn something about reporting.

But apparently you think you have the right . . ."

"*Right?*" shouted the woman. "You should talk about right! You're talking to your parents, Waldo. We *gave* you that name . . ." Waldo started to interrupt. It was impossible. The woman was under a full head of steam. One eye seemed to bulge from the pressure. It bulged in Waldo's direction. ". . . and parents have the right to do anything they please! Parents can visit you when they feel like it and parents can turn on the alarm and stick it in your ear if they feel like it . . ."

The man said something obscene.

". . . and parents can tell you that you've done a pretty rotten thing by running out on us like that. Just after you got home . . ."

"Just when you're supposed to be a good citizen and everything . . ."

"What does being a good citizen have to do with it? I'd like to know . . ."

"Well, we wanted to know a lot of things, too! But it took us nearly two days to find out that you were here. And that Doctor Watermain was pretty flip for his own good."

"For one thing, a good citizen doesn't do anything until he asks somebody . . ." The man started, but he was interrupted by the woman who was still steaming.

"What was it he said? Something about we've done enough already . . ."

"Maybe you have! Did that ever occur to you?" Waldo was backing across the room to a pack of cigarettes.

"Well, we're going to do more!"

"Why don't you *leave!*"

"Why don't you shut your mouth, Waldo," the woman said almost quietly as she started to lapse into something related to a senile whisper.

"You have no right to talk to us like that," said the man, Waldo's father.

There was silence. Then, after a few moments, the woman said, "No, he doesn't," and that was all that was said for about four minutes. Waldo had finished his cigarette and was thinking about taking another one. The man and woman remained approximately where they had been when Waldo first heard the alarm clock. Waldo was the next to speak. He spoke with no emotion.

"What do you want?"

"Listen to him," said the woman. "He wants to know what we want."

"I heard him."

Waldo saw that another outburst would not stiffen their stupidity into intelligence. He waited. Waldo knew they were helpless in the room. They hung in the room nodding, though not in unison. The nodding seemed to be a rebuttal to Waldo's silence. Waldo knew that sooner or later they would realize how pathetic they looked. They would use that.

"It's nice of you to ask what we want," the woman said, not sarcastically, but stepping gingerly into the lukewarm bathos that Waldo had expected.

"Yeh," said the man, still nodding.

Nothing more was spoken. Waldo's mother burst into tears. She sobbed. Waldo resolved privately to show no emotion. He smoked.

"Your mother's crying, Waldo."

"I see her," said Waldo.

"You should be crying, too."

"What about? What's this all about. Will you please tell . . ."

"Grammy's dead."

"Grammy's *what?*"

"She never came back!" the woman sobbed. "My own mother! She never came . . ." The sentence was jumbled by more sobs.

"*Now* are you happy?" asked the man.

"Happy? Should I be happy that she's dead?"

"Are you satisfied now?" the woman managed. "Go be a college student now! Say something *wise* now! Ha! You can't, can you?" The woman taunted Waldo with her finger and repeated, "You can't! You can't!"

"Look at him. That fixed him, didn't it?"

"Dead," said Waldo. He shook his head. He sat.

"We're gonna be gone too, Waldo," said the man. "You won't like that, will you?" Then, the man turned to the woman and said, "He won't, I know he won't."

Waldo looked up at the man and woman for a little while. Both of them were out of breath. The woman's hands were to her mouth, the man's hung limp near his pockets. Waldo started for the door.

"Where are you going?" asked the man. When the woman saw that her son was leaving she sat on his bed and placed her head in her hands.

Waldo turned to say something, but he checked himself. The man did not move. He listened to his son's footsteps slowly dying out on the long staircase that led down from the attic.

Waldo's first thought was to break something. He looked for a back window to smash, but found none, although he walked and walked, climbing over fences, cutting through back yards and flower gardens. When he saw a dog leap from behind a barrel he tried to corner it, to kick it to death. And he thought of smashing a bird with his fist. In one back yard he kicked a stump and it fell, but it was rotted and it barely rolled. It would have fallen anyway. When a boy passed him he thought of pushing the lighted end of his cigarette into the boy and, when the boy fell, stepping on his face.

But he did nothing. He asked the boy where the girls lived and if the boy knew a girl named Mona. He had forgotten her last name.

The boy said he was new.

Waldo walked toward the Chameleon.

*

"When it gets too much," Morris said, "I take my glasses off. What's eating you, Waldo?"

"I don't know. Nothing."

"If you don't wear glasses, learn how to duck. Then no one can touch you."

Waldo agreed, thought of Grammy. Ducking wouldn't have helped her.

Four students walked over to Morris. Waldo recognized the two girls. He had seen them the first day in the Chameleon. One girl, with just a hint of a nose, spoke to Morris.

"So, who's your friend, Morris?"

"Waldo," said Morris pointing, "this is Piper Kraft, Angel Kramer, Wally Dagel, and Dove Watershed."

"So you're Waldo?" said the woman called Dove Watershed. "You owe me a month's rent, in advance."

"Dove's always talking shop," Angel Kramer said to Piper Kraft. "Isn't she a perfect *find!*"

To the amazement of all Waldo extracted a wrinkled lump of money from his pocket. He placed the lump on the table and it fell apart. There were many bills in the pile, and many denominations.

When the persons standing around Waldo saw the amount of money they spoke at once: Angel Kramer said that Waldo could buy and sell Dove Watershed, Piper Kraft insisted on calling it filthy lucre, Wally Dagel said he always wanted to know whose picture was on the hundred, Dove said she would take the rent, Morris gagged, fingered a bill, and said that anyone with that much money was in Fat City.

Waldo gave Dove her money.

"You're new here, aren't you?" asked Wally Dagel.

"Yes," said Waldo.

"Have you seen Marguerite, Morris?" asked Wally again.

"No," said Morris. "Take off."

"Sure," said Wally and he left with Angel, Piper, and Dove who had put the money into her brassiere.

"That's how he makes friends," said Morris. "He asks you an easy question and when you answer it he asks you another and another. As if he's really interested. So you tell him all the answers he's dying to find out and before you know it you got a one-man quiz show on your hands. You can't shake him off. He's a misfit. Who wants a misfit for a friend?"

"He probably just wants to talk to someone."

"Exactly."

"So that makes him a misfit?"

"If no one wants to listen. That's when you're a misfit. When no one listens."

"That's when you *sound* like a misfit," said Waldo. "That's not when you *are* a misfit."

"Same thing," said Morris.

"Everyone thought my grandmother was a misfit . . ."

"I had a grandmother once," said Morris. "I'll tell you about her sometime. It's a very funny story."

"Mine just died."

"Well, that's what I was going to say. The real funny part comes when my grandmother is in her casket . . ."

At the moment, thought Waldo, what I really want is a

nice simple girl, white as an aspirin, that likes me.

"How come we never see that Mona girl around here . . ."

*

Morris led the way up the stairs and into the living room of the house. Six girls sat facing a plastic ukelele and a hand. They sang.

> I don't believe in
> Frettin or grievin,
> Don't mess around with strife . . .

"What do you want?" asked one of the girls looking up and tossing her head back. Her long hair, loosened, cascaded over her face. A chin remained.

"Mona."

"She's upstairs." The girl minced to the stairs, bellowed for Mona, then returned to the now silent group of girls. She suggested they sing "The Party's Over" and was pummeled with the plastic ukelele and the hand. The rest of the girls cheered and clapped.

"Speaking of *par*ties . . ." one girl began, but the girl called Mona was coming down the stairs slowly and Waldo never heard the rest of the sentence.

When Morris introduced Waldo to Mona the little dry house that roosted inside Waldo suddenly had a new occupant; the new occupant was busily sweeping and dusting and freshening up the place.

But there was great confusion in the little dry house. And when Waldo tried to think of something to say all he managed was, "Pleased to meet you. Maybe you remember me. I saw you goosed on the bus a few days ago."

"That's marv," said Mona. "But I'm awful about people's

names." She touched Waldo lightly on the sleeve and laughed.

Waldo became a big hand, every inch of him reaching and swelling toward the girl called Mona. He trembled, rocked on his heels and took a long look.

Mona was first of all little, nice, cute — she was so cute, Waldo felt like raping her — and quiet. She stood before Waldo, her bare feet slightly apart. Waldo, the human hand, stared at her helplessly. Her arms were bare, her legs bare, and her neck . . . bare. She was so sweet, so white, so simple and so little that she may as well have been naked.

Mona said she had to go upstairs for a minute; she'd be back in two shakes.

"She can be had. But I never did," Morris said almost sheepishly. Then he laughed. One of the singing girls saw him laughing, stopped singing, and joined him, although she had not heard what he said. Both Morris and the girl laughed and coughed. Morris stopped laughing when he looked at Waldo's face. The girl continued gasping with glee.

Waldo sensed light before him. He looked in the direction of the glow. It was Mona. Waldo was surprised to find that she was just as lovely as before she left. And when she returned the long-handled brooms started going to and fro inside Waldo once again.

"I feel silly today," said Mona. "I get these moods. I call them my silly days, isn't that a riot?"

Waldo tried to shrug, but there was so much activity going on inside him he found it impossible.

Morris said, "We might as well go." Then he looked at his wrist and saw that there was no watch on it. He said, "It's getting late" just the same.

"We might as well, said Waldo.

"Yes," said Mona, "we might as well go."

*

Waldo felt like talking to Mona when they arrived at the Chameleon, but Morris was drawing on the tablecloth with his thumbnail and Mona was watching, absorbed. Waldo watched Mona. Morris said he was drawing a tumor, a gummy tumor. Mona laughed and Morris continued drawing his tumor.

"See, what I'm going to do is write one of those advice columns in the newspaper. I know all about tumors and glands. You take someone that writes he's fifteen and he's in love with the television repairman. It's not love really. He has a tumor somewhere that's squeezing something that makes him love the TV guy. They say that mothers are ruining the country. Well, that's a big lie. It's the grandmothers that are ruining the mothers. Grandmotherism is the real problem . . ."

"Why don't you cut it out," Waldo said.

"Why don't you go hug a balloon," Morris snapped.

"Please," said Mona smiling like a demure referee, "stop fighting. I think you're both right. Now let's change the subject."

There was a long silence until Mona herself offered a change of subject. "You know, my father is really great. We do everything together. He's the gentlest man in the world."

"You're lucky," said Waldo.

"Have your parents visited yet?" Mona asked.

Waldo squirmed. "Sort of. They went back."

"They sound just *wonderful,*" said Mona.

"Maybe they are," Waldo sighed.

"I'm sure they are," Mona said. "*Mine* are."

"I haven't got any," said Morris. "I used to live with my grandmother. All *she* did was slurp her soup and drive me nuts."

"Where are you from?" Waldo asked. He thought of

Grammy slurping her soup and how she would slurp her soup no more.

"A room," Morris said. "When I wanted to talk to someone I used to call up the telephone operator. They got nice voices but I never met one. For a thrill I used to say swears over the phone and talk dirty and then they'd hang up. The TV guys used to come and give me cigarettes and shoot the bull. They were always fixing the TV or the phone or something while my grandmother just slurped her soup. She had to slurp because she had no teeth. She had them pulled. No teeth, no cavities, she said. So she called up a carpenter to make her some wooden teeth like George Washington had."

"What did he do?" Waldo asked. He was getting interested in Morris once again. He thought of Grammy's dandelions.

"He laughed and then he made my grandmother repeat it five times so that everyone in his store could hear it. He said they wouldn't believe him. Then he hung up. So my grandmother went back to her soup and I went back to the telephone operators. I still call now and then for practice. I never got out of the habit anyway."

"Your grandmother sounds like a remarkable woman," said Mona.

"She was a tumor," said Morris. "On me. At her funeral I slammed down the cover of her casket and laughed. There wasn't anyone there so no one saw me until the embalmer heard me laughing. He asked me why I was laughing. I said that I had just thought of something funny. He said I should be praying for my grandmother. I asked him why. He said if I prayed for my grandmother, then when I died I'd meet her. I laughed because who'd pray for *me* when *I* died? He said my friends. I said that the telephone operators didn't know my name so they couldn't pray for me, and neither did the repairmen. He said I was a fresh kid. At least I don't go around putting juice in dead people, I said. He said it was his job and then he called the police and had me put in a home. For laughing at my grandmother. They acted as if she could hear me. They all did. And that's the story of my life. Until some bastard laughs at my funeral. I wish I knew who it was. I'd punch him in the mouth right now."

Waldo looked quickly over at Mona. He thought she would be able to comment on Morris's story. Mona was tapping on the table with her fingers and staring across the room to the far wall where a boy sang a song. It was about his green love in the yellow wood. Mona tapped her fingers in the wrong rhythm.

"So put *that* in your newspaper," said Morris triumphantly, looking at Waldo.

"Christ," said Waldo. "You really were an orphan."

"You missed the point. What I was trying to say was *I wasn't an orphan.* I had parents. But *they* didn't know it. Those are the best kind of parents. They don't get in your way, they don't tell you to put your rubbers on, they don't tell you not to smoke. I could hang up on them if they did. Now that I think about it, I had a very happy childhood."

Mona turned. "I'm so *glad* for you," she said.

Morris said he had to leave.

Waldo said he had to make a phone call. He found a payphone and called Clovis Techy. Clovis said she was upset. She felt like a zoo. Could Waldo find one? Waldo said he thought there was one nearby.

Mona rapped on the phone booth.

Waldo was forced to make the sound of a kiss over the phone before he could hang up. It took two tries to get it right.

"Let's *go*," said Mona. "I've been waiting for hours."

*

In the exact center of the Rugg College campus Waldo stood with Mona. It was dark. There was one light burning in Boreal Hall. Probably, Mona explained, a machine that had not been turned off for the night. The mist rose off the surface of the campus pond and the whole night was moist with the fog that was trapped in the Amnion Valley. Waldo and Mona were in this envelope of moisture. Waldo's hand was touching, but not holding, Mona's.

Waldo had expected to hear insects, grasshoppers perhaps, droning, rubbing their hind legs together in the warm evening. He listened. There was no sound.

Mona suggested they walk to the edge of the pond. The soles of Waldo's tennis shoes squeaked on the slick grass. Waldo pictured himself a germ, scrambling along a wet intestine to mate. If, Waldo thought, germs mate.

Waldo took off his jacket and spread it on the embankment. They sat on the small patch of dry cloth and listened to the slurp and gurgle of the water. Mona said that the sound was the water against the edge of an enormous plastic bag which prevented the pond from trickling away.

Waldo told Mona that he felt as if they were in an envelope, licked shut, in a bottle, between two waves in the middle of the ocean.

Mona told Waldo she thought he was sweet.

Waldo started to say that he wanted her very much, but the slosh of the water against the edge of the plastic bag at their feet prevented Mona from hearing him. Mona sighed and said that she could stay in that one spot forever.

Waldo huddled closer to her and looked beyond her to the darkness, composed it seemed of trillions of tiny black threads. Waldo leaned over and kissed her.

"I could stay here forever and ever," Mona breathed.

Slowly Waldo slid his hand across Mona's stomach. He

kissed her again hoping to distract her away from the hand
creeping ever so deftly up her ribs.

Then Mona screamed. She leaped up and started picking
at her skirt.

"Oh *goodness*," she said in disgust.

"I'm sorry," said Waldo hiding his left hand.

"It must have wet right *through*!"

"Wha . . ." Waldo looked down at his spread jacket and
saw a large wet grass-stain where Mona had been sitting.
Next to it was another large dark moon. Where Waldo had
been.

"It's my new one, too. The pleats are *all gone!* That's a
crying shame," Mona lamented.

"That's what it is," said Waldo staring at the two large
patches of wet on his jacket.

*

"How's Mona?" Morris asked. "You get much?"

Waldo sat down on his bed.

"You get much?" Morris repeated. He was eating an apple
and made loud apple-chewing noises.

Waldo said nothing.

Morris paused to swallow everything in his mouth, then he
asked Waldo again, very clearly. Waldo looked at his jacket,
then dropped it on the floor.

"I found this when I got back. Someone must have kicked
it under my bed," Morris said after a while. He threw a box
wrapped in brown paper on Waldo's bed. Obviously Waldo's
mother had left it.

Waldo picked up the box. He considered throwing it out
the window at the streetlight below, but Morris wouldn't
have cared. He recognized the handwriting on the top.
WALDO was printed in pencil. He waited, then quickly tore
off the paper.

There was a blue shoebox under the paper. Waldo sat with his back to Morris and examined the contents. In the box was a plastic six-inch ruler with a pencil sharpener on the end. There was also a package of eight yellow pencils, four brownies, a tiny useless notebook; a refillable ball-point pen was in a smaller maroon box along with a matching automatic pencil, a tie clasp, and a money clip in the shape of a dollar sign. On the bottom of the larger box, wrapped in tissue paper, were some tea bags, a large pink eraser, two pairs of neatly folded orange stockings and, for some reason (a reason Waldo easily guessed at), a half a piece of chalk.

Waldo waited and soon Morris laughed and fell snorting to sleep. Then, he took the watch that Clovis had given him and placed it together with the contents of the box in the freezing compartment of the refrigerator in the hall.

Chapter Eleven

The next day Waldo sat on the grass with Morris looking at
a cloud that looked very much like an eyeball going slowly
through the sky trailing its optic nerve. Then from a great
distance another cloud followed and that one looked like an
eyeball, too. The second eyeball was catching the first; two
big white eyeballs with a man in each one shouting and pointing. But the men could do nothing to stop the eyeballs and
they collided, gently, the puffy white eyes crossing, spilling
the occupants, mouths first, onto Waldo.

Waldo leaped up, got his balance, blinked, and then sat
down.

"You're nuts," said Morris.

"Thought I saw something."

"Thought you saw something. Sure. Like Mona?"

"What's wrong with Mona?"

"Nothing. I just said, maybe you saw Mona?"

"She's all right."

"She's been had."

"Who hasn't been had?"

"But she's been had up and down and she still doesn't know
it."

"Maybe she doesn't care."

"Maybe she doesn't care. I'm no authority on caring. But
if you don't care about caring, then you don't care period."

Waldo thought about caring. He cared about writing. He

wanted so bad to be a writer, with a felt hat, a pipe, his photograph on the back cover of the book (a typewriter helpless under his hands). He cared about Mona. A nice simple girl, Mona. If the grass had not been wet the night before they would have stayed there forever or at least an hour. Waldo looked up for the eyeballs in the sky but they had gone. Off in the distance were the hoarse cries of birds and on the ground Waldo noticed the shadows of a flight of birds shooting darkly across the grass. He looked up just in time to see one bird make a frightened asterisk in the sky. It rose erratically from the top of a tree and disappeared in an arc behind the Chameleon.

"At least she's better than the other ones," said Waldo.

"That makes her boss? Because she's better than Piper Kraft?"

Waldo looked into Morris's eyes, but all he saw was himself bent across Morris's glasses. "At least she's got a nose."

"Who's got a nose?"

"Mona."

"That's funny. I never noticed. See, only a couple of people at Rugg have them — or maybe you haven't noticed. I never looked at Mona's nose so I assumed she didn't have one either."

"She does."

"Maybe that's why you like her so much. You and her are the only ones with honkers. There's a clinic in Amnion that takes care of people's noses and things. It's usually the first stop when people come to Rugg. First you get your ears chopped and then you get your nose hacked. They call it a nose job. And if you're a girl you can get stuff put into your boobs. I think they put in foam rubber or something. I asked a girl one time how they do it — she had a huge set of knockers. She said, well, you know how they put jelly in jelly doughnuts? I said yeah. She said that's how. But I really didn't know how they put jelly in jelly doughnuts so I still don't know how they do it."

"No wonder all the girls here are pretty! They've all been operated on!"

"They look okay, but the first year it aches like hell. It's one year of earaches, noseaches and boobaches. So they don't generally get had until their second year because it would hurt so much. Imagine climbing all over a broad with stitches and bruises. That your idea of fun?"

"So what happens?"

"Don't ask *me* what happens. I suppose you just take what you get. There are a lot of switch-hitters around. Why stay in left field?"

Waldo thought of those ripe girls he had seen at Rugg. Sweet little things chirping at each other through red lips and constantly waving to someone a hundred yards away. They had little flowers pinned to their big breasts like those rare mountain daisies that only grow at the top of unscalable cliffs where the air is thin. And after a session at the clinic they go to their little rooms alone to ache like hell. The surgeon's knife had replaced the fingers of lovers tracing and prodding the erogenous zones; every delicious inch had been worked over by a surgeon stitching, cutting, stuffing foamy cushions into their bosoms where only unwilling fibre had been. The shrinks screaming through their trimmed ears and emptying their heads and giving sex a bad name. And those flat-chested, big-nosed neurotic girls were normal before they knew it. Waldo saw three pass and yodel to someone far off; they hugged their books against their Firestone breasts and ran into a building. Waldo thought how easy, how hilarious it would be to make a story about all of it. *Make a story?* No, he would not have to *make* a story. He would just have to start telling it and then stop. He wouldn't have to change a word, not a word.

Waldo liked the idea. He would be a reporter, which nowadays was the same as being a real writer because everything you could report would naturally seem like fiction. What Jasper Pistareen had called "sweaty stories." That's what it would be. And here he was, Waldo, boning up, learning how to report. After he found out how to report he would write it all down; and then if all the human interest stories were scrambled up a bit they would call it a novel. Change a few names, bumble up a few places; the real with a grin would become the surreal. But if reporting was just saying what you saw, just telling it, why go to college at all? It wasn't like Booneville where you had to get your papers to get out clean.

"What about college?" Waldo asked.

"What *about* college?"

"When does it start, what do we do?"

"You're here, aren't you? You want to *do* something?"

"I'd like to find out about reporting. I want to —"

"Journalist, isn't it? You want to be a journalist?"

"That's right," said Waldo. "I want to write stories."

"So write."

"You mean, start in? Write?"

"Yah, start in. Write. How else do you expect to do it? Unless they have one of those machines that write for you. Machines that tell stories."

"I'll write," Waldo said.

"Write about broads. Everyone writes about broads. Except make it a little different. Write about dwarfy little broads that turn up here and there, ones that have been had."

"Are you talking about anybody in particular?"

"No," said Morris. "No one in particular."

"But I can't just write about girls."

"Then write about boys," said Morris, irritated, "write about faggots and queens, write about yourself, that's what everyone writes about, don't they? Or write about Fred, there's a book for you. *Fred Wolfpits, Professional Shit*, you can call it."

"I thought you liked him."

"I do. What's wrong with being a professional shit?"

"Nothing, I guess," said Waldo.

"You should meet him."

"You keep saying that."

"Yah. If you want to, you will. You'll never meet anyone in your life like — "

*

"I collect Orientalia," said Fred Wolfpits. "As well as a good bit of Occidentalia."

Neurotically enough, Fred Wolfpits looked like a Negroid goat. Large flaring nostrils, a kinky beard, and claws at the ends of funky hands drained of color. The beard seemed composed of light filaments; his face was a strange brown-yellow, jaundiced with evil like Erratio Lizardi's. Fred was one of those people, Waldo considered, one of those rare people who did not look as if he lived under water. Most people looked like that, like they lived under water, scrubbed and red. But Fred looked as if he lived under a rock.

He wore black. A cape, thong sandals, and when he puffed on a cigarette he squinted through the smoke. He looked a little like a magician, a Negroid, slightly goat-like magician. Waldo pictured Fred pulling a rabbit from a battered pocket, producing a rabbit from two old eggs; the rabbit was making mewing noises and had a tiny cloven hoof that it was trying to hide.

"Are you interested in Orientalia?" Fred asked. He stared

at Waldo, his eyes like pale blue marbles, not blinking, freezing all the stuff in Waldo's body: the brain, the little house, hands, props, and so forth.

"I don't know," said Waldo.

"You don't know if you're interested in Orientalia?"

"I don't think I ever saw any," said Waldo.

"He doesn't think he ever saw any," said Morris.

"I heard him," said Fred. "But perhaps he is interested in Occidentalia."

"He's interested in writing," said Morris.

"You don't say," said Fred. Fred looked at Waldo and said, "Are you interested in Occidental or Oriental writing?"

"Accidental writing?" Waldo asked.

"Enchanting," said Fred. "Where did you find him?" he asked Morris.

"On the thing," said Morris vaguely.

"I'm at Rugg to study reporting," said Waldo.

"Which kind?" said Fred, meaning Oriental or Occidental.

"Just reporting."

"There is no just reporting," said Fred, "but I am glad you're studying reporting. I'm something of a reporter myself."

"No kidding," said Waldo.

"No kidding," said Fred pursing his lips. "Here's a little thing I wrote on that movie actress that passed on a while ago. I was living in Colfax, California, at the time. That's where I come from."

"I come from a room," said Morris.

Fred Wolfpits rummaged through a folder full of press clippings. He had written them all, he said. He told Waldo to sit down, and he held a leaf of paper in his strange fingers and began reading: "Dateline Colfax. In death as in life, Bella Feenix — you remember Bella Feenix — drew a throng of curious fans. New paragraph. After the mausoleum had been closed and the mourners had departed, the curiosity seekers — held back from the star's funeral by the police — streamed up the road of the quiet cemetery —"

Fred read in a very somber voice. Waldo looked at him again, at his clothes. No, not a Negroid goat, not a magician. Fred was an undertaker; now speaking in a low voice of one of his recent undertakings.

" — they pushed and shoved their way to the vault, trampling the flowers that lined the steps in front of it. The women in colorful capri pants and bright sundresses and the men in summery — there's a good word, summery — sportshirts. One man and woman wore swim suits. A good touch, no? Anyway," Fred continued reading, "they ripped the flowers and the ribbons from the sprays, including the huge heart of red roses sent by millionaire ex-hubby, Lenny Goldquid. The crucifix from Miss Feenix's half-sister, Mrs. Augie (Hap) Walzer, was knocked down and walked on. New paragraph, the grabber, you see: a woman, asked what she would do with the ribbon she had filched, said she would preserve it in a glass case!"

"Literature," was all Morris said. He took a big swig from a bottle.

"That's Occidental reporting," said Fred, "Bella was the biggest bang in Colfax. Of course, I have lots of others." He found another clipping, a very small item. "This one is charming. Listen, I call it *The Sting of Death*. Walter Phocine, 49, was stung to death by wasps yesterday. Doesn't that one crack you up?"

Waldo's mind stomped back on the rungs. Yes, the voice was familiar; he had heard it before, had seen that dark suit before. Waldo tried to recall where.

"Do you ever go to the Mandrake?" Waldo asked.

"I used to," said Fred. "Used to work for delightful old

man named Jasper Pistareen. I don't do much for him these days what with being at Rugg and sniffing airplane glue and making LSD in the Chem Lab. I'm hoping to write a novel one of these days. It's just a matter of getting high and writing obituaries. Here's a good obituary I wrote last year." Fred picked up another piece of paper and began reading.

Waldo looked around. He noticed that the room was very neat, or rather, the trash in the room was collected into very neat piles. In the center of the room, near Fred, were two stacks of newspapers. On the wall there were many pictures, including a full color picture of Bella Feenix stretched into an arabesque, smiling, nude, reaching perhaps for her clothes. There were piles of incense and fat gonadal Buddhas, jars of seeds, joss-sticks, a black fez, ticket stubs and many, many newspaper clippings. There was something on every flat surface. All the articles in the room seemed about to close in so that the room, coffin-shaped, was like a great vise composed of nothing but small pieces of junk. Orientalia, Occidentalia.

"— and Sherbert Gaff, inmate of the Booneville School for Delinquent Boys, gave up the ghost," said Fred finishing.

Waldo looked at Fred. "Did you say Booneville?"

"Yes, they lost one a few months back."

"I know," said Waldo. "I was there."

"You were in the *pen*," said Fred, brightening, as Jasper had brightened when he learned that Waldo had been in jail.

"Yes," said Waldo, "in the pen." And then he thought what magic that word had brought to him. Nothing seemed very special about jail, about Booneville, when he was there, he thought. But now what magic it made! It was like saying he had been to college. Waldo thought about this a moment and then he said, "And now he's dead."

"As a duck," Fred said.

"Yes," said Waldo. Waldo felt a wheel in his heart turn and yank on a cord. The cord was attached to his throat, and he felt himself strangling. He coughed. "So you're a reporter. You really get around, don't you?"

"I get around, I get in. If you want to be a reporter you've got to crawl inside people's heads, crawl through the debris. Especially if you're doing the human interest bit."

"That's what I'm really interested in," said Waldo. "I'm interested in human interest."

"Delightful," said Fred Wolfpits.

"Fred," said Morris, "is loaded up to his ass in human interest."

"Morris is so anal," said Fred. "That's because he's impotent."

Waldo glared at Morris. "Mona said the same thing. In fact, Mona said Morris was the most impudent person she's ever met."

"Enchanting," said Fred.

"She's been had," said Morris.

"Are you sure," said Fred, "you want to be a writer?"

"Sure," said Waldo.

"How about that?" said Morris.

"Anyway," said Fred, "how do you like Rugg?"

"I like it all right."

"You're a talky little bastard, aren't you?"

"You asked me if I like Rugg. What am I supposed to say? I like it all right. All right?"

"But you seem a little uninterested."

"He does," Morris interjected.

"Seem uninterested? It's a place. I've been places before."

"Yes. You were in the pen, weren't you?"

"That's right. If I hadn't been there maybe I would think this is a great place. But I've been in the pen so what does it matter what kind of place you go after that? It doesn't make any difference. I really don't have to go to college. I been in the pen."

"In the pen," Morris sneered across his lips, "in the pen. What's the goddamn pen!"

"The pen is the pen," said Waldo.

"And you think this is another pen?" asked Fred.

"I don't know," said Waldo. "Do you?"

"Well, I have my collections of authentic Orientalia and Occidentalia and knickknacks. I do a little writing off and on. I even write dirty little things for filthy little magazines, but they don't pay much — I'd be a lot better off if they paid by the orgasm instead of the page, but they don't — oh, I keep busy. I like to keep my fingers in everything, so to speak."

Morris giggled.

"I see," said Waldo.

"So it really doesn't matter what Rugg is like. I don't notice it much and it doesn't notice me — or, I should say, us."

"Me and Fred," said Morris.

"Well, that's nice you collect all these things. But I don't collect anything," said Waldo. "So I get bored easier than you do."

"You don't collect *anything?*" Fred asked, astonished.

"No, all I want is a nice simple little girl and a job on a newspaper — say, that man Jasper's — and a little money."

"What do you want the girl for?"

"What do you mean *what for?* I just want one, that's all."

"And when you get her and put the boots to her, what then?"

"I don't know."

"I'll tell you. Two things can happen," said Fred. "Number one you might find out you're let down. Nothing is so overrated as a good screw and nothing so underrated as a good crap. You'll get mad and beat the nice simple girl to a pulp for thinking otherwise. Or two, you'll meet someone and instead of you picking up that someone, the someone will pick you up and won't let go. And there you'll be, howling your brains out in the air. That's the difference between people and things. People — friends, especially — are bad for the complexion. Give me my knickknacks any day. It's safer."

"There's no money in it," Waldo said.

"Where does that put me?" asked Morris who had been listening wobbly-headed with drunken intensity to everything Fred had said.

"You're a great big knickknack," said Fred, "and you're very sweet."

They kissed. And then they fell to the floor of the narrow room and began clawing each other and making little braying noises.

When Waldo saw that they weren't paying any attention to him he started to walk out of the room. He walked by the nude photograph of Bella Feenix and read the inscription: "For Fred Wolfpits who made me what I am today; the most loyal friend a girl ever had, Eternally Yours, Bella F. . . ."

Chapter Twelve

"*Duck,* Dove!" squawked Gull Watershed.

Then there was a series of loud crashes, the screech of brakes, and the tinny plink-plink of glass dropping onto the street.

Waldo woke up, ran to the window and looked down.

Clovis Techy's white Cadillac was parked diagonally across the lawn of the boardinghouse. The tire marks made disastrous little paths from the street to the lawn. Near the street was a squashed barrel which had squeezed forth wads of trash. And on the lawn a plastic flamingo lay shattered, his body in pink slivers. The whole collection of the Watershed animals had been run over by Clovis. The inflatable ferret lay punctured and flat. The lawn was strewn with counterfeit viscera.

Waldo looked hard. Clovis had not gotten out of the car — she was still behind the wheel and appeared to be laughing, but Waldo was not sure. While Waldo was making up his mind about whether Clovis was laughing or not he glanced back and noticed that for the third morning in a row Morris was not in his bed . . . Waldo thought for a moment of the two out-of-breath knickknacks on Fred's floor . . .

"*That took a lotta brains!*"

Waldo looked out again. Dove and Gull Watershed were walking toward the Cadillac. Clovis got out. She smoothed her coat slightly and then assumed a very cool posture near the car and smiled demurely. Clovis had that look that advertisers seek — whenever Clovis stood still she seemed to be advertising something, as if whatever was near her could have been on sale. Except today, Waldo thought, she appears to be selling money . . .

Waldo's head jerked forward. Clovis had a fistful of money which she held slightly behind her. It seemed to be running through her fingers and down her white coat.

"This is gonna cost you plenny," said Gull angrily.

"Plenty of what, love?" asked Clovis still posing.

"You know damn well what I mean," Gull said trying to be gruff but unable to overcome a certain cracked sound, the squawk which was native to his voice.

"I beg your pardon," said Clovis smiling.

"I hope you got dough."

"Why you rough man," Clovis laughed. "Are you threatening me?"

"No," said Gull. The crack in his voice exposed great stores of fear. "But them animals cost dough."

"You mean this?" Clovis raised her arm and stood tall, holding her fistful of money as if it were a torch. Deftly she let the bills fall from her raised hand one by one. The bills fell from her gently moving fingers and flapped to the ground lightly where they caught on the mangled animals.

Gull and Dove, seeing the statuesque Clovis bravely freeing her money, said no more. Their arms flew out straight like base-stealers and they skittered about the yard whimpering before they finally decided to lunge for the pieces of green curling in the wind.

Caught in a crossfire of laughter they swayed and swooped for the bills. Gull scratched for them. Dove went nearer, directly to the source of the currency, and gathered busily.

Clovis seemed to be enjoying the scene immensely; she watched the married couple bowing and scraping for the eva-

sive pieces of money, trailing easily from the flaking green
torch. It was the kind of scene that is best accompanied
by double-takes, cowbells, cymbals, pratfalls and Sousa.
But Clovis had now stopped laughing and was getting bored.
Her arm dropped to her side and she watched no longer with
amusement. She was disgusted. She shook her head and
threw the money as hard as she could into the wind. Both
Gull and Dove darted for the same bill, cracked their heads
and rolled on their backs, feet in the air.

Clovis looked up at the brown house and frowned. Waldo
waved, but Clovis did not see him. She started for the front
door.

"I'll be right down!" Waldo yelled.

Clovis did not stop. She continued walking up the front
steps and disappeared under the roof of the front porch.

Waldo dashed for his pack of cigarettes and dumped out
three. He was vainly trying to light a match when he heard
Clovis on the stairs. He smelled the familiar perfume and
heard the whispering of her straw shoes. Outside he heard
Gull and Dove chirping on the grass. There was a rustling
of satin and stockings — all the sounds that announce a
woman — and then, Clovis Techy.

"Waldo!" Clovis cried. "You're still alive!" She dug into
her purse and came up with five wrinkled twenty-dollar bills.
She handed them to Waldo, mumbled that it was a present.
and then began to undress in her curious way. Instead of
taking things off she unzipped, unbuckled and unsnapped;
soon she turned away from Waldo.

Meanwhile, Waldo tried to stuff the money into his pockets.
But he had no pockets. He was naked except for an unlit
cigarette which, however much it dropped from his lips,
would not droop enough for modesty's sake. Waldo arranged
the money into a fan and covered himself.

Clovis turned. She smiled. And then slowly she drew

open her coat as if it were the curtain to a cozy little theater-in-the-round. She nodded for Waldo to enter, which, with his fan, he did. Clovis closed the curtain around him and pressed all her nakedness against him. The money-fan fluttered to the floor and the matinee began.

*

Clovis still felt like a zoo. The Bethesda Tesh Zeitgeist Memorial Zoo was off-campus. Waldo wheeled the big car into the parking lot. He looked up and saw a group of buildings: a baby-minding service and nursery, a gift shop, a bar, a booth complete with lawyer for the convenience of those who wished to name an animal they had grown fond of as a beneficiary in a will, and a florist ("Fauna Florists").

The Bethesda Tesh Zeitgeist Zoo was an authentic reproduction of a thirteenth-century monastery which still partially exists in southern France. Partially, because most of the original stone had been broken from the foundation to help build the zoo. To make it convincing. There were high walls all around the zoo with tiny windows and ivy, passageways, cloisters, and a subtle Muzak which played only Baroque music. There was a belltower on a central cathedral-like building.

Clovis explained that this building with the imposing belltower and the heavy oak doors was the Monkey House. They entered and saw an indignant mother wrenching the arm of a small boy. The woman was wearing what looked like a gymsuit, blue, with a ruffle of a skirt which stuck out a good four inches. Except for the straw hat with the built-in sunglasses the woman could easily have passed for a gymnast.

The boy cried as the gymnastic mother pulled him away from the cage. In the cage was a baboon standing erect, thumbs around the bars, staring like a condemned prisoner.

The little boy pointed toward the inflamed root of the baboon which appeared from a swatch of blue hair at the anthropoid's groin.

Near the back of the Monkey House a rhesus monkey contemplated the act of life with his mate, bored and consumptive-looking, while picking his teeth. Clovis and Waldo did not stay long in the Monkey House, for although it was large and contained many cages, it smelled. The small monastery windows did not admit much air. On top of all this Clovis insisted on sneaking up behind Waldo, tapping him on the shoulders and, when he turned, gluing kisses on him and laughing out loud.

Outside, Clovis walked over to a cage where a beaver first splashed for the viewers, then gnawed green paint from the steel bars of the cage. Waldo pointed to a cage filled with sawdust. In that cage, their pink flesh just peeking out of the sawdust, were baby white mice. They looked like many clean thumbs. The mother mouse sat in a corner meditating on the heap of sawdust and babies.

"They just hatched," said Clovis.

Otters, ptarmagins, emus — all either eating or glowering. Eagles, egrets, wasps. Owls roosting under hoods and leaves. The braying of asses mingled with the assured cooing of doves. Gaggles, clutches, bunches of animals and birds together like sullen mutineers. Great-flecked horned things with hooves and beards; mudhens being buggered by cocks; lazy big-tongued things licking each other.

"They look real," said Clovis.

Waldo agreed.

The shriek and tattoo of birds, cages vacated and moldy, cages teeming and stuffed with fur and straw. The whole spectrum of animal life squawking from the hutches and pens at Waldo and Clovis. And passing among them they

viewed all the continents, all the rivers, all the steppes —
even the underview of the stones and shells; the majestic
and the microscopic. The entire trip through evolution,
starting with color plates in one of the chapels and ending
with the woman with the straw shoes, naked under her white
coat and the boy with a pocket full of twenty-dollar bills
edging toward the SHOOTING GALLERY sign.

At the far end of the zoo there was a series of cages with
people lined up in front of them. Each person held a rock,
a bow and arrow or a pistol. Some merely held green apples.
A vendor nearby wearing a white suit and a baseball hat had
the word AMMO embroidered on his chest. He was saying, "Try yer luck."

"Try yer luck," he said to Waldo and Clovis.

"What are you selling?" asked Clovis.

"Ammo," said the man. "Say, you look like a big strong
feller. Whyancha try yer luck?"

"With what?" asked Waldo.

"This here's where they dispose of the old ones. Mangy
ones and such. Take yer pick. The bigger the critter the more
ammo you need. Costs most to bag a lunky horse. You can
squash a rabbit for two bits if you're a good shot. See, this
way the zoo don't have to do it, and more people come to
watch and try their luck. This is a big zoo so there's a lot of
mangy animals that got to be chucked away. A good Sun-
day and we finish the whole mess. Weekends is our best
time . . ." The man broke off to sell a whole armload of
ammo to a family.

The people were having a wonderful time. One boy was
taking careful aim at a cornered buck. The buck finally
rushed at the boy and, as he did, the boy shot an arrow into
the twisted mouth of the buck. The boy's fiancee mooned
and ahhhed when he did this. A few arrows later the buck

lay in his own blood and a curtain was rung down as the corpse was carted off. A boar hog with curling tusks and a skin disease was pushed into the cage.

Up and down the cages children were pitching green apples, rocks and arrows at the screeching, dying animals.

"I thought you gave the animals to museums when they got old," Clovis said to the ammo man.

"Used to," said the ammo man. "But the market value ain't so high. God, we get our best prices for the big ones, giraffes, and hippos. Ever try to bag a hippo? You try some fine day and see how far you get. Why, I seen *acres* of ammo thrown at one hippo. Took the damn thing three weeks to kick off. Families came here — big families — night after night. The hippo kicked, of course, but people said it wasn't the ammo that did it. It was nothing but sheer starvation. If we'd sold that old hippo to a museum we wouldn't have gotten beans for it. As it was, we cleared a few thou in ammo alone."

"You want to try your luck?" Clovis asked Waldo.

"I'm not in the mood," said Waldo.

"It looks kind of awful. But I don't suppose I'd mind lobbing something at a wart hog. Look!" she said quickly, "They're even selling poisoned darts!"

The ammo man heard her. "We got everything," he said.

And yes, thought Waldo, they certainly did. But this is what the whole thing (life) was about. Man had come a long way — now he had little pockets where he could screw his knickknacks and lob rocks at sick animals. What made it all rather special were the velvet ropes that surrounded the people, little aisles and circles that the people hopped around in doing this and that. Suddenly there was a place for everyone, a neighborhood where he could go about his business — even if his business was only writing sweaty stories and then reading them to his friends. If there was a secret it was in finding the right neighborhood where you could do what you wanted, where no one would bother you. Then anything you did would be very important. And as long as you stayed in your own neighborhood you would be okay, you might not even die. Or if you did, if you did die, then no one would slam down the top of your casket and laugh. You killed the animals in the zoo — nothing icky about that if the deaths of the animals were necessary to make you feel good.

It made Waldo feel good to have figured this out; but it bothered him too, because he hadn't figured out where *he* was supposed to be in all this. He wasn't looking for a road-map to take him to the right place, but wasn't Clovis sort of a fleshy roadmap that would take him where he wanted to go? Oddly enough, Waldo had the distinct feeling that college wasn't everything it was cracked up to be. Rugg wasn't red hot and this wasn't the place Waldo wanted to spend his life. If he was to spend his life among the knick-knacks they would have to be in a pretty special neighborhood. And if Booneville, Rugg and the Bethesda Tesh Zeit-geist Memorial Zoo weren't the right neighborhoods he still had the pleasant feeling that he was a lot closer than he was before.

"Duck!" said the ammo man bringing Waldo back to the B.T.Z. Memorial Zoo Shooting Gallery once again.

A rock whizzed past his ear and hit the retreating shape of a small furry thing. A woman giggled and a whole family ran to the bars to see what damage had been done. One saw blood. Someone said he was lying. Another rock. "*That's* blood," said someone else. And Waldo walked away.

Clovis had gone on ahead. When Waldo found her she was standing with a whole group of people near a big cage.

Waldo pushed toward the front of the cage. Clovis nodded to him when she saw him, but kept looking at the occupants of the big cage.

In the cage were two elephants, one trumpeting after the other. The cage was circular and around and around in a heavy swaying dance they went. Soon the one in front became tired and knelt in the center of the dust. The one in back waved his huge hose of a trunk and blew a trunkful of dust at his partner. Then he parked his two feet on the back of the kneeling elephant and with a lot of trumpeting and a lot more dust and trunk-thrashing began stabbing the kneeling elephant in a hard gray crack under her tail.

Waldo turned to the people. More had gathered. One man was gasping for breath; he was a small dry man and he was squeezing his popcorn box in his little bony hands. Several people snapped pictures and one man cracked his knuckles in rhythm with the stabs of the second elephant. A boy and girl held hands and gaped. Then the girl looked at the boy's hand in disgust, dropped it, and pressed her hands under her armpits. What amazed Waldo was the perfect silence, the reverence of the people all feeling their hands. Maybe it was fright. Whatever it was, it certainly was silence and the only real sound was made by the elephants which, according to the shiny front of a little girl's portable radio, had now become one six-legged hill of hard grey skin. A rather inefficient hill at that; full of waste motion, billows of dust and random noises.

When Clovis left, Waldo followed her. She went straight to the bar which was located in the cloister of the zoo. She hadn't said a word until she had two drinks, and then she said, "You want to know why people come to zoos? I'll tell you. They want to see the animals laying each other. They always do it naked and they don't care if you watch."

Later, though not much later, Clovis asked Waldo if there was a motel near Rugg.

Waldo said he thought they had passed one.

The little blue-haired lady at the desk did not mind when Waldo said he had brought a friend. She knew about college students, how they gallivant around and sow their oats. That's what Waldo heard her telling someone as he paid his money and left the office.

In a jiffy Clovis was ready. Waldo looked over at the bed not dreading what was going to happen, but not looking forward to it. It still hurt a little bit. Waldo almost trumpeted as he slid into bed. Outside in the hall someone (probably the blue-haired lady's son) was squirting bug spray out of an aerosol can; the faucet near the bed dripped, while someone in the next room rapped on the wall in time with a piece of music that could only be heard as a beeping drone. The person in the hall paced back and forth rhythmically squirting; rain started and dripped from the eaves, and cars — two hundred in single file — splashed through a puddle outside the window, front wheels, back wheels, front wheels. It all irritated Waldo. He got up and turned on the dripping faucet full. The water gushed into the sink so hard that a fine spray reached the bed.

"There you are," said Clovis.

Chapter Thirteen

"I've missed classes," Waldo thought to himself when he awoke the next day at four in the afternoon. He extracted a long hair from his mouth and looked around. He was in his own room. Morris was not there. Waldo looked out the window and saw the sun. Soon the sun would set. Waldo had not been outside. He pulled his clothes on and went outside and walked down the street toward Mona's boardinghouse. Strangely, Waldo felt ill. It was the trees. There were big blossoms, red-streaked white napkin blossoms on the trees. They gave off the sickening smell of cheap perfume; so did the other flowers, the ones in the neat little beds. Waldo's head reeled; he fanned his nose. And the sun setting was like someone many miles away who had chosen to torment Waldo with a large mirror, shining a blazing light into his eyes. Waldo squinted at it and had to turn away. He felt faint and walked behind a house where there was no sun. It was cold out of the sun, damp, and still the flowers gave off their two-bit smell. Toilet water, thought Waldo. Waldo felt sick. He could not go on. He went back to the Watershed and up to his room where he sat on the bed until Morris came in.

"Where have *you* been?" Morris asked throwing a whole stack of books on his bed.

"What about you?"

"I went to classes," said Morris. "I admit I might blow

lunch before the end of the semester, but it's the only way you can stay at Rugg. Go to classes now and then . . ."

"I got other things to do."

"You might blow lunch."

"So what? I got friends," Waldo said thinking that Clovis had friends and that her friends were his friends. "I don't need anybody."

"Well, you been in other pens before, so you know all about pens, don't you?"

"That's right. I was in the real pen. I was there for a long time," Waldo said. For a moment he had trouble recalling what he had been put in prison for. Then he remembered and did not bring up the subject again.

There was a long pause. Morris finally said, "Fred's thinking of having a party. He wants to know if you want to come."

"Who's he inviting? The rest of his knickknack friends?"

"So you don't want to come?"

"I'll come."

"Tomorrow night. Fred's."

"I'll be there."

"You don't need anybody, isn't that what you said?"

"Not a soul," said Waldo.

*

Mona looked up. Waldo stood before her, out of breath. Mona looked at him blankly, as if maybe she had seen him before, her eyes slowly focusing.

Waldo lifted her to her feet and kissed her, edging over to her and finally squeezing her against him. When Mona screamed in his mouth Waldo let go.

"You frightened me," said Mona. "You really did."

"Let's go someplace else," said Waldo snatching Mona's wrist once again.

"You're so ferocious!"

Waldo laughed, but could not seem to continue laughing. He jerked Mona's wrist. "Come on," he said. "Let's go someplace."

"No. Yes. Let's go someplace and then we'll go someplace."

"Okay," said Waldo, "but let's hurry up." Waldo took Mona's arm or, rather, slid his hand from her wrist to her arm. They walked to the Chameleon.

"Let's sit over here," said Waldo seeing a small table near the wall. Mona sat. When Waldo looked at her she began, without the slightest effort, to smile, like a flower, a well-upholstered odorless flower. Waldo reached for her stem.

"I feel silly tonight," said Mona looking around the room. "You ever get these silly moods? All these people. Sometimes I can't stop laughing."

Waldo withdrew his hand. "Let's go," he said.

"Lots of people," said Mona. "Lots and lots. You ever notice? There are some people that *really* look as if they're enjoying themselves. Like that boy over there." Mona pointed to a boy who had his coat over his head and was pretending he was a ghost. He bumped a table and elbowed some students who were dancing. He limped through the room shouting under his coat. He was drunk.

"Let's go," said Waldo.

"He *really* looks as if he's having a good time. Boy, he looks like a lot of fun."

"Who looks like a lot of fun?" Waldo asked quickly, looking up.

"That boy over there. The one that just knocked the other boy over. The one that's talking to the other boy."

"You mean, the one that's pushing the other boy?"

"Yes. The one that's fighting there."

"Him? *He* looks like lots of fun?"

"He looks like *loads* of fun."

"He looks like he's *loaded* to me," said Waldo.

"It's really crowded tonight. It isn't usually this crowded. But it's really crowded tonight. I say *really* a lot, don't I?"

"Let's gooo!"

"Hum?"

"Let's go somewhere."

"Okay," said Mona. "I was just watching these people."

"They're having lots of fun," Waldo said, getting up and leading Mona out of the Chameleon past the people struggling slowly around — puny things saddled with loads of just plain fun.

"They sure are."

Without too much trouble Mona and Waldo sneaked up the back stairs of the Watershed. Waldo's room was seedy. Mona paced around like a rat in a maze. Then she started picking up Waldo's clothes.

"Look," said Mona, "I'm domestic!" She laughed but stopped laughing when she saw that the clothes that she was picking up were the ones that Waldo was quickly taking off. She sat down on the bed glumly, or as glumly as one can look in a darkened room.

"You didn't want to come?" Waldo asked. "You didn't have to."

"I don't know. I guess I'm in a silly mood tonight."

Waldo sat next to her and gave her a little kiss on her fist which was clenched against her cheek. It was as close as he could come to a peck on her cheek, a peck on her fist.

The streetlight outside gradually made Mona's face visible. Next to the top of her fists were her eyes and they looked quite vacant. In fact, her whole face, pressed between her hands, seemed white in the darkness, empty, the only empty thing in the room, as if whoever had been in her head had now sneaked off and was somewhere else.

"I really didn't want to come here," she finally said.

"We can go," Waldo said falling flat on the bed and drawing Mona down. She keeled over stiffly, her fists still against her cheeks, knees still bent. Waldo shoved her into position but she would not uncoil.

". . . it's just that I don't know, someone says do this or let's do that and it's usually a lot easier to do it because if you say you don't want to then the next thing you've got to do is give a reason. That's the hard part. I can never think of reasons for *not* doing things so I usually do things. Get it?"

This frightened Waldo a bit. It was something he had often thought about. That was *him* talking. You have to live a long time before you know what not to do and so you find yourself doing everything, or at least trying. And if someone threw something at you you had to duck or take it in the ear. No need to fight back. And giving reasons — Mona was certainly right there. It just used up time. Who could think of all the reasons? Who could believe all the reasons once he thought of them?

Waldo looked over at Mona. She was still coiled up and still talking.

". . . and one time I asked a guy directions. I was on the subway traveling light, no map or anything. He said he knew the exact place I was looking for. He said he'd take me there. So we got off the train and walked outside. He was sort of a guide — that's what he did all day. He waited until people asked him something and then he took them where they wanted to go. The city was big, he said, and most people were too busy to help and give directions. But not him. So we walked a few blocks and pretty soon he said, Well I live right here — we might as well stop in. We stopped in. It was his house, you see. An apartment house. And there we were standing in front of his house. I mean, *it was his own house.* He wasn't lying. He had the key. We went upstairs and when we got into his apartment he made me a drink and then said, what's a little girl like you walking around the streets alone for? I didn't know the answer to that one. I wasn't little and I was going someplace. I told him, I was going someplace, until he took me to his house. So I said, I don't know. Then he went over to the door and locked it and pulled down the shades. I said to myself, well, what's going to happen now? Although I knew. He went around to all the rooms and checked if there were people inside and then came out and said, *where did you say you were going?* I told him. That's right, he said, I remember you telling me. Then he nodded his head and said, Well, there's an easy way to get there and there's a hard way to get there. Now, which do you want? Naturally, I said the easy way, if it wasn't too hard. I had the feeling that the easy way was hard. Then I got an idea and said, easy for who? He said, both of us, that's who. Let's go, I said. Wait a minute, he said. So I waited a minute and he didn't say anything. I'm in a hurry, I said, so what do you want? To do what I tell you, he said . . ."

Mona's voice droned through her fists. She seemed to be getting tired just telling the story. Slowly her fists unclenched and her body began to relax against Waldo's. Her mouth was now pressed against Waldo's shoulder and she spoke into his shirt.

". . . but I can skip the next part — although there isn't much left. He said, take your clothes off. I told him no. He said, then what did you come to a strange man's apartment for? That was a good question, wasn't it? I thought you were going to take me where I wanted to go, I said and I watched him come toward me. I did, he said, and then he laughed. He laughed like a car starting up. Then he drank down his drink and looked at his watch. We better get going, I haven't got a heckofalotta time, he said. Then he said, you're not a virgin anyway. Which was the truth — don't ask me how *he* knew, but it was the truth. I might as well, I thought to myself. So I didn't even say no. I just took my clothes off — most of them but not all — and I thought of where I was going and I kept thinking: *this is one way of getting there.* It was over in a few minutes. He was only too happy to let me get dressed and pretty soon we were back on the street walking like before and you know what?"

Waldo's mouth was dry. "What?" he croaked.

"Well, he took me to *exactly* where I was going. He even paid my bus fare. I *never* would have found the place alone. I was even a little ashamed because I thought he wasn't going to take me there after all. I thought I was going to be a dead duck, all raped and everything. When we got to the place, he said, see, here you are, easy. I took you exactly where you wanted to go. It was true. Then he asked me my name. He said he wanted to take me out on a date. But I said, I don't give my name to strangers, sorry. He laughed — not like a car starting but a nice laugh now. I said, maybe we'll meet on the subway again. Sure thing, he said, sure thing. He smiled. Then he walked away."

Waldo held her hand and wished with all his heart that Mona was rich. Then he slid his hand off Mona's and touched her cheek. Mona looked at him, opened her eyes wide in the dark and said, "Oh."

That was all. It was an *oh* of surprise, but after she felt his full weight her expression seemed to say, "Well, here you are, just like the others" or "Welcome aboard, I hope you enjoy the trip." She looked at Waldo's face. Her gaze stopped there. It did not enter his head.

Waldo found it quite difficult to unbutton Mona's blouse.

He scrunched around the bed and saw the reason he was having difficulty: Mona was quickly taking off her clothes, interfering with Waldo's inexpert attempts to help. She took off most of her clothes, but not all of them.

Waldo knocked his elbow against the wall, contorted himself into position and then began disproving every sexual episode he had ever read. At least Clovis knew what she was doing. A lot of things happened just like in novels, Waldo thought, but this (he looked down at Mona) isn't one of them. Nothing was happening on Mona's face. Her eyes were open, staring at the ceiling, past Waldo, like those of an insomniac.

At one point Waldo said, apropos of nothing, "I love you."

"I love few, too," Mona replied softly.

After a while Mona closed her mouth and sighed through her nose and so Waldo knew that it was probably over with her and that it was not love and maybe not even, well, lust.

Chapter Fourteen

Waldo entered a large oyster and met two woman who said they needed him desperately. We need, need, they chanted; but Waldo brushed them aside and said that he didn't need anyone because he had a lot of friends. The two woman became a crowd, reached for him, and threw him to the gooey floor of the oyster. When Waldo tried to breathe he felt his mouth fill with a pasty substance that gagged him like a mouthful of noodles.

When Waldo woke up he found he was sucking on his fingers. He got out of bed, remembered that he was at Rugg College and that classes were beginning (since by his calculations it was Tuesday morning), dressed, took his pencil, his rubber eraser, notebook and half piece of chalk and went outside. The flowers still made him sick. The blossoms on the trees bothered him. Waldo ran down the street as fast as he could, up past Boreal Hall to the classrooms. When he saw a room full of students he went in.

Waldo was relieved to see a map on the wall. A history course, Waldo thought. The map was in full color with tiny names in a long list at the side. The mountains were red, the plains orange and yellow with rivers of cobalt blue. The Louisiana Purchase, of course. The shape was certainly familiar. The Mississippi Delta was unmistakable. Waldo traced his hand over the smooth map. It had been a long time since he was a student, a long time since he had sat with a blank paper in front of him ready for all the notes he would make on it. Maybe school wouldn't be so bad. Waldo looked at the map — so intelligent and at the same time inscrutable. The thought occurred to Waldo that perhaps he would like school, perhaps he would like Rugg College and perhaps he would stay and stay as Fred Wolfpits stayed.

Then the bell rang and the professor walked quickly into the room and slammed the door. "Now *there's* a boy who's really taking an interest in this course . . ."

Waldo smiled and started for his seat. He was trapped in a canyon of legs. Someone laughed out loud.

". . . let's hope," the professor said through his nose, "that he does not take too active an interest in what he was just doing. I am referring to his careful study of our new color-plate of the female uro-genital system!"

Waldo found a seat in back and the professor began his lecture. He was a tired-looking man. He looked as if some-one had beaten him up, roughed him up in the corridor just before the class began. He shuffled back and forth in front of the class. He spoke about how you get the name biology, how it is really two words and not one. And then he talked about life and about the exams they would have every month and how people thought that science was no good and why they were barking up the wrong tree. He riffled the wrinkled papers on the desk and moved on to the universe. Then he inserted his little finger in his ear, fished around for wax and said, "This may be a digression, but if I were going to give God a grade on the Universe I'd give him a C-minus . . ."

There were only two more classes that day, journalism and anthropology. The professor of journalism had a felt hat tilted back on his head, his tie pulled down and his feet up on the desk. He was pushing short sentences and gutsy prose. "Give it to the reader below the belt. Make him understand

what you're getting at right off. No fancy frills. No kid stuff."
He waved his arms. "If there's blood, say so! If someone's
dead, where and how! Get acquainted with *alleged* and you
can't go wrong . . . "

When the class was over Waldo took a long look at the
professor of journalism; what intrigued Waldo was the hat
the man was wearing. It was a journalist's hat, the kind with
a deep brown stain on the part that touched the man's head.
It was crushed and sweaty and faded and looked authentic.
The hat rose and went out of the classroom.

Waldo followed the hat into the corridor where it disappeared among the milling students. Waldo stood on his tip-
toes to get a look at the hat. And then he saw another hat
enter the Men's Room.

When the classbell rang and the students trickled slowly
out of the Men's Room, Waldo entered. His reflection in the
tiles made hundreds of rippling Waldos on shiny squares. He
spotted the hat, holding a mop.

Waldo walked up to the hat. "Is that yours?"

"Is *what* mine?" answered the hat in a human voice that
seemed both old and soft as felt.

"The hat. I want to buy it," said Waldo.

A man emerged from under the hat. He startled Waldo a
bit at first, though his features were not too much different
from the features on the hat — wrinkles, stains, ridges, the
whole face squeezed in places and bulging in others, discol-
ored and drooping. People can get to look like their dogs,
why couldn't they also get to look like their hats, however
old hat that might seem?

"There's a story that goes with this hat."

"I just want the hat," said Waldo, "not the story."

"My wife gave me this hat . . ."

"Five bucks," said Waldo.

". . . she's been dead six months."

"Ten," said Waldo.

"No," the man said wagging his finger, "*six*. I should know."

The man went on. His name was John. John's wife was the greatest little woman in the world, rest her soul. John knew her as a child. They grew up in Amnion, lived their whole life there — or at least she did. They played there and, after John got out of the army, got married, and that was that. No two ways about it. Now she was dead. Could she cook? She could cook like a house afire. But now John had to go back to his black house at night and cook himself.

"That's rough," said Waldo, "cooking yourself."

And he could hear himself cooking, John said. The funny — not really funny, but odd — the odd thing was that he, John, made all the noises in the house now. He said that Waldo would never know what it was like to make all the noises himself, *all* the noises. It's something you don't think about until it happens and when it happens it's damn scary. When you stop making the noises there's no sound at all, none.

"Twelve," said Waldo, "for the hat."

Sure, John went and told the doctor all about it. But what can doctors do? Doctors couldn't bring his wife (her name was Gladys) back. John hoped that Waldo didn't mind him telling him all about it. Except that she was such a peach of a woman. Always laughing, fooling around, until *bing* she died. Before you could say . . .

"If you want to keep the hat, just say so. I wouldn't blame you a bit."

It was not such a nice subject to talk about — death, not Gladys — but the doctor told him it would be good to talk about it. It would do John a lot of good to say the words:

she's dead. Dead. Not a bad word if you say it enough times.

But apparently John had not said the word enough times because John was crying now and saying the word over and over hoping that it would not be the same, hoping it would soon, Waldo assumed, mean nothing. But apparently the word still meant something because John was still crying after several minutes of saying the word, although the doctor said it would be good for John. And the hat, now in John's hand, was dotted with John's tears that had plunked onto it and made tiny black stains.

Waldo pictured the doctor teaching John to say dead. The doctor was saying, "Go ahead, John, it's good for you!"

John said he should talk about it more often, every chance he got. She was dead and gone, dead and gone. Waldo didn't mind hearing the story, did he? After all, she was dead . . .

"I don't want the hat any more," Waldo said. "You keep it. I'll get another one." Waldo looked at the hat. It was perfect. A reporter's hat.

. . . and gone, John repeated, staring at the hat.

Waldo opened the door and started to leave.

When John noticed Waldo leaving he rushed up to him. "Well," John said grasping Waldo's hand and shaking it, and even smiling, "it's been good to know you, son. I'm sorry you had to hear the story — I know you must hate to hear about dead people. But I can't help thinking about it. All part of getting old, I guess. Ha-ha. Anyway, the doctor said that it's good for me to — "

My God, thought Waldo while he was walking down the corridor, on top of not getting the hat I missed anthropology class!

'Gobble, *gobble*, gob-ble! Happy, *happy*, hap-py!"

Waldo turned. It was Mona.

She sang and rolled her head: "Guess who's having a party

tonight, guess who's having a party tonight, guess who's — "

Waldo steered Mona outside. She was attracting attention in the corridor and Waldo was sure that she would start soon on Happy Birthday and Olly-Olly-Infree.

"What's on your mind?"

"Nothing, really," said Mona in her normal tone of voice. "Fred Wolfpits is having a party."

"I heard. Will it be any good?"

"Good? Good? that Fred," Mona's eyebrows jigged, "his parties are wild! I mean, others are just smacky-mouth, finger-bowl and drink-a-few-chills. But Fred's are fab! And Fabby Fred's having one tonight."

Fabby Fred, Waldo thought. He had never seen Mona so excited, so incoherent. But this was the party he had been hearing about since the first day at the Chameleon. Waldo figured he might as well try it. Morris turned out to be gay, the flowers stank; Rugg was a no-fun Booneville and Mona a well-used jukebox that, for a small coin, would play tales of fat and naked cities in which those lost citizens traveling light on subways met for a brief hour of smacky-mouth.

"He's the only great man I know," Mona went on. "Fred. He leaves the room and he's gone for two or three minutes. Then Morris introduces him like on television. And Fred, well Fred stands there and gives speeches on accidentals and dung piles and how civilization is up the creek and we're all lost souls, very Christ-like and well-meaning, and no one cares about anything any more like God and Freud; they're just interested in money, money, money. No one cares about love and goodness and how beautiful it is to see a small naked man feeding pigeons with crusts of bread."

"Fred Wolfpits seems like quite a person," Waldo said. But all Waldo could think about was the two struggling knickknacks on the floor of the coffin-shaped room.

"He's very Christ-like," Mona said, "and he knows all about God without sounding big-mouthed and whuddayacallit. He's terrific, Fred. And when he gives these speeches everybody gets drunk and sings folksongs about this land is my land and your land. I don't know. It's just the greatest bunch of people I've ever known. They're *real* people. You'll see for yourself."

"I hope so," said Waldo remembering that he must call Clovis and tell her about it. She liked parties.

"You know how it is. People are only looking for one thing."

"Yes," said Waldo thinking of Mona's encounter on the subway, Morris's encounter on the floor, Clovis's in back seats and wet motel rooms, the elephants with an audience and so forth.

"Money. Everyone's looking for money or something, everyone's got big ideas. But these people at Fred's parties. They're not looking for anything; they don't have any big ideas. And they're so *funny*. I mean, in a sad sort of way. Everything's like that. Funny and sad, crazy. But marvy sometimes really — sort of tragic and stupid." Mona stopped for a moment. Then she raised her eyes to those flowers Waldo detested so much and said, "Life, it's heart-rendering."

*

Fred Wolfpit's face. Behind it a Mount Rushmore of faces, luminescent-yellow in the queer glow of Fred's coffin-shaped room. Fred takes a reefer from his dear drained lips and shows his fuzzy light-filament beard. If he is Christ-like then perhaps it is Christ between the ages of twelve and thirty-three. The one that stays well off the pages of the Gospels.

"You're late."

"It's not even dark yet."

"Late-shmate," said Mona.

"It's got to be dark before you go anywhere?"

"I didn't say that. I said Morris was vague about the time."

"Let's go *in!*" pleaded Mona waving: a raised eyebrow each for Piper, Angel, Wally, Morris, Gull and Dove.

"You didn't say Morris was vague about the time. You said it's not dark and that's why you didn't come sooner."

"Stop *ar*guing," said Mona. "Let's go in."

Fred stared as Waldo brushed past him. Morris, next to Fred, remarked that something was a good joint. He was holding a tiny cigarette.

Waldo walked over to a table and poured himself a drink. The room was filled with bodies and faces; but the bodies did not seem to be attached to the faces. Everyone Waldo had met the previous week at Rugg was there, and there were many more he did not know. Morris was still talking to Fred, Piper Kraft had cornered a foreign student that appeared to be wearing his pajamas. Gull pecked at Dove, Dove cooed into Gull's ear. Wally danced merrily with a hulking girl wearing a lumberjack's shirt, blue jeans and hobnailed boots. Waldo waved slightly at Wally. Wally broke away from the girl and came up to Waldo.

"Hi there," said Wally brightly. Wally was hairy, had bulbous eyes and was very small. He reminded Waldo of a horsefly. "You haven't seen Morris around, have you?"

"I just saw him talking to Fred."

"Is *Fred* here?"

"Fred lives here," said Waldo remembering Wally's angle of approach.

"Of course," said Wally.

"Who's that girl you're with?"

"That's Marge," said Wally drawing his mandibles sideways.

"That's Marguerite." Wally leaped into the air and yelled, "Margue*reet!* Hey, Margeee!"

The large girl lumbered over to Wally on her hobnailed boots. She bounced her head once and placed her hands on her hips as a greeting to Waldo.

"Pleased to meet you," said Waldo. He noticed that Margie had a moustache.

"I don't know about you, but I need a fix," said Marguerite. "I'll see you later." She stomped away.

"So long Marge," said Wally, but Marguerite did not turn. Waldo asked Wally her last name. Wally said it was Baggsomething. He had forgotten the last part of it, but he knew there was a hyphen after Bagg. Wally explained that Margie wanted peace at any price; she had participated in sit-ins, eat-ins, lay-ins, fly-ins, walk-ins, and talk-ins. She was in trouble with the campus authorities because she had repeatedly refused to shave off her moustache.

"She's a big girl," said Waldo finishing his drink.

"I like 'em big," said Wally softly, "and brassy. I don't know why really. I suppose it's because I'm not domineering enough. The truth is, I'm usually domineered . . ."

"You mean dominated."

"Yes. Sorry. Dominated. Can I get you a drink?"

"Okay," said Waldo. Waldo overheard Gull and Dove Watershed telling some people about the woman that crushed their animals. It was Gull, they said, that did the trick. He had demanded cash on the spot and the woman literally threw all she had and ran she was so flustered.

Wally returned with the drink. Waldo sipped and saw that Marguerite Bagg-something was with several other boys. He assumed that Wally was a sexual comma rather than a period for Marguerite.

Wally was lonely. Wally drifted away to a corner and absentmindedly opened a closet door. Inside were a boy and a girl wrapped among the brooms making love. Wally giggled and shut the door; he went over to Fred and said, "No skeletons in *your* closet, are there?"

"No," said Fred pursing his lips. He walked to the back of the room. The next thing Waldo heard was a squeaky voice saying, "Getcha han's offa my tool!" Then there was silence.

Nearby, Gull and Dove had stopped talking about Clovis and were now pinching and clawing each other to show how married they were. Dove started telling everyone in a very loud voice what Gull did at night to her, how perfectly Henry Milleresque he could be. Gull shushed her and smiled a bit devilishly, though no one saw him except Waldo.

Piper Kraft applauded Dove. In fact, every time Dove opened her mouth Piper applauded, until finally Dove gave up talking and Piper told every one that she herself adored Gull's ascot — so much better as an affectation than Fred's fuzzy beard, and no trouble to keep clean. She then introduced everyone to her foreign student friend.

Gull asked if it was true that Africans were still anthropophagists.

The African said that sometimes anthropologists lived in the villages, but they mostly wrote books about boughs, bids and brasslets.

At this point someone suggested that Piper Kraft liked foreign students because she collected stamps. The African looked blackly at the speaker and walked away.

A boy in a seersucker suit, seedy with gyzym, mottled with nosebleeds and lipstick-smeared, sidled up to Piper Kraft who was telling the Watersheds that they should definitely work on a *kibbutz* if they went to Isreal as planned. It had been a wonderful experience. No. A real joy to see all those people in their natural habitat. The boy in the seersucker suit was grabbed off by Marguerite Bagg-something. Marguerite told the boy that she had been hyphenated by incest.

The boy in the seersucker suit was not listening to Marguerite. He told Piper Kraft that the *kibbutz* bit was a bore. All you had to keep in mind when abroad, he said, was that the successful traveler is bilingual and bisexual.

Waldo walked over to Morris. Morris said that he was glad Waldo could make it. Waldo, emptying the glass in his hand, realized that he might be drunk. He said that this was the biggest pen he had ever seen in his life and he didn't care what anyone thought because he didn't need anybody. It was at that moment that he began looking for Clovis.

He passed Fred who had walked up to Wally and was poking his forefinger into Wally's tiny ribs as if he were pressing the doorbell to an empty house. Waldo heard Fred say that Wally was a maggot. Fred looked at Waldo and asked Waldo what he was looking at. Waldo said nothing.

Waldo walked away from Fred and saw Morris again. He was about to say something to Morris when a voice from the back of the room called Morris the biggest asshole that ever lived. Morris's face looked like an apple that was quickly ripening and then rotting — all in the space of a half-minute. Morris's large lenses, nacreous with angry cornea, shuttered once in Waldo's face as Morris began looking for the person. Morris saw no one except Dove Watershed darting her pink tongue through her lips at the foreign student. Then, in a manner of explanation, she said that she had read someplace that it was a very sexy thing to do.

Marguerite announced that she would use telepathy on Angel Kramer to tell her to leave the boy in the seersucker suit alone. Marguerite stared until her eyes watered. Angel didn't even notice the giantess with the hyphen. Angel held

the sleeve of the seersucker suit and watched Wally fastening
Fred's cape around his waist. Jane Austen-like waltzing, per-
verted somewhat, yet still rather formal, she explained to
the boy in the seersucker suit. Wally continued to dance
with Fred and Morris continued to look for the source of the
voice.

Very politely, almost too politely for words, the African
student asked Marguerite what was in the punch. Marguerite
told the boy that it was fruit punch, gin, and plum juice.

Piper Kraft and Angel Kramer turned sharply and accused
Marguerite of being anti-Semitic. Marguerite told both of
them to screw. Hearing this exchange, Mona began looking
for Waldo, Fred dropped Wally, let him ping-pong through
the room looking for a friend; and Fred looked for Morris.

Waldo, drunk, thought of neighborhoods and Grammy.
From a certain angle Marguerite reminded Waldo of Grammy,
tough, though lacking Grammy's best qualities. Marguerite,
he was sure, would never be able to say to her grandchildren
that she was steady as a clock, cheerful as a cricket and busy
as a bee. He looked at Mona. A nice simple girl was all he
wanted, white as an aspirin; Mona looked back at Waldo. She
twisted her mouth into the shape of a swear-word as Clovis
had once done. But Waldo was disgusted. Clovis was a
grown woman. She knew about things like that. Mona made
Waldo very sad, just as all the people in the room made Waldo
very sad. They were happy and they had nothing to be happy
about. What did they know about looking for the right
neighborhood? How could they be so sure they belonged
there? Waldo looked again at Mona and wanted to say something to her. But he caught himself and said nothing when
he realized again that she was not rich.

Fred came up to Waldo and told him that he personally
had rescued Morris from an orphan home after Morris had

slammed down the top of his granny's casket and got in trouble with the embalmer. He said that although a lot of people said he was a professional shit, Morris had turned out to be a professional queer, liked it a lot, and they were now made for each other. Like a cork in a bottle, he added. Then Fred went over to Morris who had dropped into a chair and put his bristly beard on Morris's head and nuzzled Morris affectionately saying, "You little bitch, you squirt, I shouldn't waste all my energy on such a little squirt . . . mmmmmmmmppppppffff . . ."

Waldo thought only of the six-legged elephant machine he had seen at the zoo. He avoided looking at Mona and found himself in between Piper Kraft and the boy in the seersucker suit. Piper told of her near-rape in Naples by a sweaty travel agent who had also called her a plump Jewess, not that it mattered much, and her father's dealing in US Army surplus, canvas and rubber goods, in exchange for Tel Aviv, gay Paree, Roma, and Milano and Firenze, and another quick feel in a youth hostel in Geneva — twenty-seven countries in nine days — a chain on her bike snapping, nearly breaking her neck in Flanders as she raced from the Autobahn near Friedrichstrasse to the tram in Piccadilly; Piper Kraft, watched by Waldo and the boy in the seersucker suit, sounding cheated from the bridge of her new nose right down to the chipped lacquer on a minor tarsal.

Waldo looked around and thought, I'm getting out as fast as I can: I've had all I can handle. But Waldo could not think for the life of him what the man's name was that offered him the job, the man with the sweaty stories, the one that was in the Mandrake, the jailbird . . .

The boy in the seersucker suit pushed past Waldo. Waldo watched him cross the room and enter the toilet.

And then it came to Waldo: *Pistareen*, Jasper Pistareen.

Waldo left the room and stood on the front steps of the house mentally numbering all the usable stories he had heard since coming to Rugg. Those stories were worth money to the right person, to a reporter, for example, even if he didn't have a hat. Waldo started down the stairs. It was very dark outside and the insects were making a great racket. Although Waldo could not see the flowers very well he could smell them and the smell was disgusting. Waldo figured the smell was probably greater at night since there were fewer nostrils around to take up the slack.

I'm free, thought Waldo. I'll just find Jasper Pistareen and write the stories. I have all the stories I need: The Sonofabitch Who Wanted to be President, Morris and the Dead Granny, Mona Meets a Travel Agent, John and Gladys, or the Fable of the Felt Hat, The Ammo Man, At Home with Fred Wolfpits, How to Fill A Jelly Doughnut, or the Making of Piper Kraft. Plenty of stories, sweaty and otherwise, and not excluding The Great Booneville Affair, a ballad of sugar and pain. All I have to do is leave and I'm free. Waldo felt like reporting. He looked for Clovis; she had always been there before. Waldo put his coat over his head to keep out the smell of the flowers. He peeped out of the coat. Clovis was not there. Waldo felt in his pockets. The money was not there. The reek of the flowers entered under the coat. Waldo backed up the stairs and entered Fred's room once again. And then he thought, *I'm trapped.*

Waldo sat for some time with his head in his hands. When he looked up at the people in the room he became frightened. What is it about a face that is scary? A face lurching through a room, the mouth pulled out of shape with laughter or screaming; a face mangled by glee grinning madly; the blurred faces of people hopping up and down, dancing. It was the thought that they were human beings that disturbed

Waldo. That was one thing. The other thing was the expression that each was wearing on his face. Waldo took a long look at Piper Kraft. He looked at her nose. The longer he looked at her nose the longer the nose looked; soon her body, her face shrank to nothing. All that was left was her very dangerous nose.

He went into a corner and watched. For a few moments he thought of how it had been at Booneville. He remembered being in the oven, looking out through the glass at the boys running against the invisible walls, the great Booneville affair. How simple it was to get in, how easy it was to stay in if you played along. How impossible to leave.

Trapped, thought Waldo. Otto Noon had gotten out of that kitchen, yes. By being clonked on the head by a guard. And Waldo had gotten out of the oven, yes. By getting cooked nearly to death. He had gotten to Rugg easily — Clovis had gotten him there. Almost an express trip; two stops: the Mandrake, the back seat of her car. But all in all it was easy to get places; the question that remained: *how do you leave?* By getting your skull broken? By getting yourself cooked? By paying your fare of two balls for one trip out and one in?

There were only two ways. One was having a friend such as Clovis who would act as roadmap and car for a slightly immodest but not outrageous fee. The other way out was by either dying or by coming so close to death that the pain blocked the doubt that you would ever make it alive. You could either be carried or you could suffer and go. And once you have been carried, suffering is out.

Waldo became frightened again. What if she doesn't come? If she doesn't, I will die — the hard way. The faces were making noises; Fred Wolfpits was tickling Morris and Morris was saying hee-hee-hee; Angel had the seersucker suit all to herself; Wally fondled one discarded hobnailed boot and the girl with the moustache and the hyphen was elsewhere with the African boy who insisted that he was not wearing his pajamas; and Mona, that poor thing, was sitting on the floor and looking like an aspirin that has been dropped into a tall glass of clear liquid — she was coming apart, crumbling softly into tiny sexless flakes.

Little by little the party came toward him and very soon it was only a few feet away. An unidentified arm reached out for Waldo and just missed him. Waldo drew back flat against the wall. More arms reached out and there were shouts this time. It was getting dangerous. In the crowd, above all the heads, Waldo saw the face of Fred Wolfpits. It was yellowish and gulping smoke. It looked at Waldo and grinned a mouthful of rotting teeth at him.

Waldo's body began to ache and his throat hurt. No one had actually touched him but the pain was there, caused by plain homemade fear. Waldo inched along the wall to the door and when he came to the door he looked back. The Watersheds were arguing, deciding whether they should have a baby, while Piper Kraft told them of the newest advances in birth control. Marguerite Bagg-something began to sing. Soon there was dancing in a circle. Polite applause, the subdued waving of Kleenex.

Mona pulled herself together and approached Waldo. She touched his arm. Waldo squawked. It hurt. Waldo looked at Mona. She was horrible; her mouth was the wrong shape, someone had switched her eyes while she wasn't looking, and now she couldn't see straight ahead. She gargled something at Waldo and Waldo started away. He heard, I love few, I love few. She slobbered a goodbye and then wrenched the boy in the seersucker suit away from Angel. The boy smirked and covered a nosebleed on his coat with his right hand. They began to cha-cha-cha.

Waldo bolted for the door knowing all the time that the invisible open space held a large amount of invisible but very real pain. He stood for a moment on the steps, looked at all the rotting flowers and took a deep breath. He had just about keeled over when he forced himself to look up. He saw nothing. He took another breath and grasped his stomach and had started to fall forward when he saw a glossy white Cadillac screech to a halt. It was no use. He fell in a heap.

Part Three

Chapter Fifteen

He had been in the same hotel room with Clovis for about three weeks without leaving, even for a minute. And the hotel room was not large. As a result he had spent nearly the whole time "riding shotgun," as they say in the cowboy movies. The only difference was that he was riding shotgun in bed and not on the broken seat of a wagon.

Waldo was getting good at it. Like the cowhand who sits in a broken wagon-seat for a long time he soon accustomed himself to the discomfort, then actually counted on the discomfort. The elbows in the gut and shoulders in the way, the knees in the groin, the wet mooshy feeling, the heat, the damp sheets, like the lumps in the sprung seat were part of the game. Once in a while he would get excited and stab his finger into Clovis's eye. Clovis would moan while Waldo kissed its tears (tears from one eye — that amused Waldo immensely) and nursed it. And Waldo had devised all sorts of ways of prolonging the act. He would — in the middle of it — conjure up the picture of a cow in a field which he had seen at the Bethesda Tesh Zeitgeist Memorial Zoo. The cow sat chewing slowly. And then the cow began munching a bit too rhythmically, urging the cud up and down in her mouth. It looked like the end. Clovis thrashed. The cow would get up very, very slowly, hind legs first, one leg at a time, the tail swishing. Then the cow would stand in the green field quite still. Always a little wet-eyed heifer would barrel along and try to prong the big cow. A silent eureka showing in Clovis's gaping mouth. By then, la-la-la, it was too late. Clovis had already glued a long kiss on Waldo's mouth. Waldo was inert.

So they made love all the time. It didn't hurt any more and Waldo was getting good at it, and even liked it.

Except when it was over completely. Then Waldo fell on his back and felt that he was dead or dying, every drop of life wrung out of him. He would lie still wondering what ever possessed him to begin. But it was all over. He had read where people would hold each other in their arms after making love and sigh, "feeling," the books usually said, "a delicious fatigue in their limbs." That was the part that weighed heavily on Waldo. The fatigue was not delicious. It was a deathly heaviness that pressed on him. And since all his strength had been spent he could only lie still, a prisoner to that cold sluggishness which came after. It was the price of making love and Waldo paid it every single time he and Clovis made some.

Afterwards Clovis talked about herself. She had been a child star and then, after a slight pause for puberty, a starlet.

But a star's life wasn't all roses. She had some tough times. In the snow trying to get a car out of a rut so they could make the premiere. The leading men — all of them pansies — with shovels chipping away at the ice crust while the snow dropped in big wet flakes on their heads. The child stars, the starlets, the aging actresses lined up freezing in the snow and watching their hairdos go to pieces and listening to the pansies saying that they shouldn't have to shovel the snow, one of them even complaining of an hysterical pregnancy. But this helped Clovis realize that it was all uphill before you could bask in praise from coast to coast. She had what it took and was going places and the sky was the limit, everyone said.

Of course, when you're young you just see the bright lights. You never see them fizzing out in the rain and being replaced by an assistant with dirty hands and a tall ladder. That was something Waldo could be thankful for, she said. Here he was on top of everything and whose ass did he have to kiss to get there? He would never know what it was like. Could he honestly say that he had stood in the snow while about nine pansies shoveled and bitched their way through a snow drift? It wasn't the pansies. No. It was the feeling that there you were standing in the snow, a starlet with something on the ball, and where were all those people supposed to be? The ones that clapped like crazy. Behind the trees, maybe? A lot of good the woods does you, Clovis said she thought in the snowstorm, when you have personal appearances to keep and miles to go before a genial host makes you glad to be alive. But Clovis had a that's show-biz attitude toward it all, including the making of her own starlet-dom.

"I've always been lavish in bed," she would say and nudge Waldo's mostly inert form. Waldo would swallow some saliva and nod — not because he didn't know what to say, but because anything he said when he was naked seemed to be off the subject.

Although movies lost their glamour after a while men were still fighting for her, hundreds of them (they still called her up once in a while). Short ones, muscular ones with wavy hair and class, poets — skinny, white, suicidal — artists, idealists with rucksacks and big boots, gamblers with traces of foreign accents, huddled masses yearning to breathe free, the tired and the poor, men who needed her and whom she inspired, one at a time and lavishly, to great things. Naturally, she married one of them, the wrong one, the biggest bastard that ever lived, although rich. She hoped Waldo understood her, and now he did.

Her husband enjoyed torturing her, being cruel mentally, always seeing other women and bragging about it. She hated his coarse peasant's hands, she said (his father had been in bottle caps). He took her for granted, gave her the royal runaround, sold her a bill of goods, had her, frittered away the best years of her life, had no respect for her, and rubbed her the wrong way.

And while Clovis told her tales and puffed away on the cigarette and named each man in order Waldo lay near death on the bed regretting everything with every square inch of his body, three-weeks' nakedness and his own long tale over with and wishing very much that he could meet Jasper Pistareen so that he could report something. When Clovis's memory became fuzzy she mashed out her cigarette and asked Waldo to refresh it. Once refreshed she chugged along gabbling her stories. She spoke without malice about everyone but her rich, fat-assed husband. She was not bitter about anyone or anything. She had had everything she ever wanted and at thirty-seven had had more than, she said, her share. It was only right, she had given herself, hadn't she?

Waldo, she said, had had his share too. It wasn't every boy that could boast of a mistress like that. He had been places. Probably more than a lot of kids his age. He could thank Clovis for that. Hadn't she showed him a good time? Hadn't she? She wasn't asking Waldo to be grateful, but he had to admit that she had made him what he was. And very soon she would give him a chance to be a reporter. All she wanted in return was her just do.

"My just do," Clovis would say sighing, closing her eyes and placing her hands in back of her head to fully expose in the daylight a naked body that had all the earmarks of being considerably older than thirty-seven. Waldo could tell because for one thing the skin on Clovis's neck was out of whack — it was soft and pouchy and worried looking. "Give me my just do."

And Waldo, sighing and dragging himself sideways into position for the night run all the way to East Cloaca and back for a short snooze, would give her her just do.

So many colors, Waldo thought. Indeed, the wallpaper of the room was multicolored and showed battle scenes and plantation scenes from the Civil War. There were southern ladies and gents with parasols and muskets. Waldo had been looking at the wallpaper for a long time. Now he saw that there were two or three layers of it. Teddy bears from underneath seemed to be carrying muskets, the soldiers appeared to be riding hobbyhorses and even the quality folk from the genteel plantation scenes were being showered with paper hats and streamers. It was all very interesting and Waldo stared at the wallpaper from many positions.

Food, cigarettes, and bottles of liquor were ordered through room service and promptly delivered by a bug-eyed bellhop who took goofy looks around the room as he was counting out the change. He had grown to ignore the towel which Waldo wore just as Waldo had ceased to notice the bug-eyes and the goofy expression that after a while became a grin — lacking in warmth, but a grin none the less. Waldo and the bellhop became friends. The bellhop was the only other person that Waldo had seen for three weeks; Waldo looked forward to his visits. Waldo usually gave back the change that the bellhop carefully counted out and the friendship became such that the bellhop would wink and give Waldo a Jasper Pistareen go-to-it-you-hot-shit nudge as he was leaving. The door would then slam and Waldo would lock it and turn toward his benefactor who raised her arms to him in welcome.

Waldo had other ploys to distract himself and prolong the

act besides the cow in the Zeitgeist Memorial Zoo that got
slowly to its feet. Waldo sometimes tried to estimate exactly
how much time had elapsed since Fred Wolfpits' party. This
was not only difficult and absorbing, it was — fortunately
for Waldo — impossible. There was a gap between the time
Waldo fell down the Watershed stairs with his nostrils full
of nature and the time he woke up in the hotel room with
his hands full of Clovis. It had taken several days to tell the
story of home and Rugg. He slept during the day sometimes
and sometimes at night. Sometimes he ate twice a day, sometimes three or four times. Friendly as he was with the bellhop he still never dared to ask the time. He didn't want the
bellhop to think he was getting tired. Waldo chose the figure of three weeks because it showed him to be neither horny
nor chicken; though Waldo suspected that it was much more
than three weeks. He had not been in the room long enough
to hate Clovis, but sometimes he lingered in the bathroom
expecting to come out and find her gone and her purse on
the bed. It never happened. He never really expected that
it would. And though Waldo wanted that job as a reporter
very badly the thought of leaving the room and Clovis to
look for the job never persisted. Yes, it crossed his mind, but
that's all it did. After all, Waldo was getting good at making
love. He didn't want to cheapen it.

But the color of his skin underwent a change. It went from
a vague pink to a faded yellow, washed-out at the edges. Also
he was molting. His hair had started to fall out a bit. Everyone's hair probably falls out, he thought, if they watch for
it. He took a lot of baths and became fastidious about his
nails. He had lost a little weight. He didn't feel badly. He
had a lot more than most kids his age. Still he looked in the
bathroom mirror a moment before he went to Clovis and
each time it became apparent that he had lost his bloom.

But so what? So what if he looked like something from the Zeitgeist Zoo Shooting Gallery that had just dodged a brick? So what if he happened to just find himself in love with a full-grown woman? So what if his hair was starting to fall out? And, by God, so what if he happened to like it? That's a crime? Some people hunt around for years looking for a good place to plop themselves. Here he was mostly satisfied at the age of — he forgot how old he was for a moment but he knew it would come back to him and it didn't matter anyway — and living in relative bliss for a few weeks or so with Clovis in the hotel room. He wasn't asking for much, neither was she. They were happy. Is that a crime? They helped each other in little thoughtful ways. But still both of them knew what the score was and neither of them said, "We're living a lie," or "We can't go on like this," like a lot of people might.

Sure, sometimes Clovis was hard to please. That was to be expected. She had had a lot of interesting and unusual friends; she had been a lot of places. And Waldo could only talk about the time he nearly got cooked in the Booneville Testing Kitchen or the week at Rugg. Still they were good solid stories and telling them killed a lot of time. If these stories didn't entertain Clovis Waldo had lots more to tell, lots more. Life was as simple as satisfying Clovis and if Waldo couldn't satisfy her then it wasn't *her* fault. It was his. And that was the best part because it made Waldo give his best to a woman who knew the long and short of things, a full-grown woman he could trust and who would pay him well. It was a good education, all things considered. It brought the best out of both of them.

They took turns but usually it was Waldo's turn. Waldo would go into the bathroom and dream up the wildest thing he could think of. Then he would go into the bedroom and tell Clovis. Nearly always Clovis would clap her hands and say, "Let's do it! It's worth a try!"

For example. One day Waldo was backstage in the bathroom looking around for an idea. His eye lighted on Clovis's lipstick on the sink. He picked it up, played with it a while, and went straight into the bedroom.

"Let's play school," he said.

"I want to be the *teechah!*" shouted Clovis in the baby talk they sometimes used. She had just begun to use baby talk. Before the baby talk there were several other accents they used, like French ("poot your body here and zen I weel be happee") or homemade dirty lingo ("I love your slug — put it in my jukebox and we'll have a tune") and so forth. Naturally Clovis was better at it. She had been a starlet.

"You be the blackboard. I'll be the teacher," said Waldo. He threw back the sheets and class was in session. Waldo played tic-tac-toe on Clovis's breasts. He drew faces, wrote swears, and fashioned handles and price tags and arrows all over her jiggling flesh. When he finished he stared at the numbers and arrows trembling with Clovis's laughter. She loved it. She said it was the cutest idea Waldo had ever come up with. When both of them became tired of looking at it Waldo got another tube of lipstick and turned the whole mess into clothes, a tight-fitting sticky red frock with toreador slacks. Clovis drew for a while on Waldo, then they made love pretending they had clothes on.

Afterwards Clovis said that the whole thing reminded her of a story. She had some friends who owned a swimming pool somewhere. They used to invite friends over and then sit at opposite ends of the pool. To kill time between drinks they wrote dirty little messages on their children's backs with lipstick. The children would trot to the other end of the pool where the invited guests would cream the message off and scribble a filthy reply. It was a good idea. They avoided writing about touchy subjects like politics or religion, the children enjoyed getting the sun and being messengers for their parents. A lot of kids never got to really know mom and dad. But these kids had it made.

And Waldo said that story reminded him of the Grammy story. Waldo went on to tell again about Grammy and the dandelions and the time Willy Czap was buried. Clovis loved the story. Waldo went on. He told, with some embroidery, the story of his father's love affair with the truss that Waldo later had the pleasure of burning. When Waldo ran out of stories or could no longer disguise the Booneville, home or Rugg episodes he began telling bald-faced lies. Clovis could not have been happier and she immediately gave Waldo a large tip.

The result was startling. Waldo launched into fifteen different lies about hooking green apples, swimming in the lake, chawing tobacco and catching crawdads with his bare hands, even though he had never seen an apple tree, couldn't swim and thought a crawdad was a widowed Indian.

Clovis again paid him for his efforts and this time not in kind but in money. Waldo began to think harder and soon came up with another mouthful of lies which were purchased by the hungry Mrs. Techy. At this point Waldo decided that he was an artist — a bullshit artist to be sure, but an artist. He had learned the art of reporting, and if Clovis was that grateful for a tale what would Jasper Pistareen say? And what about all those readers of Jasper's popular paper? They would pay. Waldo found it all very simple: he would continue practicing with Clovis and then he'd be all set. He realized that he owed a lot to Clovis. She was right. She had taught him everything he knew. Most of all she had taught him the value of a dollar. It was what Clovis called a simple matter of give and take — it had nothing to do with salesmanship. Either you had a product or you didn't. Clovis had spent long hours praising Waldo's productions. But it had not dawned on Waldo that he could sell so little for so much. Just taking an extra minute to hear everything that a person had said paid off in the long run. Waldo couldn't make up lies, he could only extend truth into lies by extenuating the circumstances and changing the names and fabricating a bit. Perhaps, Waldo thought, they weren't even lies, for if he had thought of them they certainly were possible. What could you possibly think of that wasn't possible? Who would have thought that a full-grown woman would take such a shine to him when his mother's left eye continued to give him a cold shoulder? If that was possible could there ever be any such thing as a lie?

With this over and done with Waldo felt a lot better about lying to Clovis — not to mention lying with Clovis — and Clovis willingly paid him for it all. It had come to the point where every time Waldo went to get a drink, every time he said something clever, and every single time he showed the slightest degree of affection for Clovis ("I owe you the world," "I don't think I could ever repay you for all you've done for me") money gushed into his hands. It is a cliché to say that every time he belched he got paid, but several times Waldo belched particularly loud and was rewarded on the spot.

Life went smoothly only occasionally interrupted by the thought that Waldo could make more money working for Jasper Pistareen's newspaper. Waldo became a whizz at making love, too. There were none of those little irritations that are characteristic of lewd old men that want a little fun. He was young. He did not have to get up and make frequent urinations (though, more than likely, he would have been paid for each one); he had no blemishes or pulled muscles to apply cream to; he didn't have a bad knee or any old army or football injuries, and he only had to shave every few days. Perfect.

Somewhere around the seventh week (according to his own calculations) Waldo noticed that his skin went plain chalky and lost the mellow tint that it had acquired a few weeks before. Tiny encrustations appeared, foreign lesions popped up all over his body, and his hair had almost completely disappeared. Great hunks and swatches of hair fell out and Waldo hid them under the mattress along with his fistfuls of money. He felt smaller, too; littler. He knew that it was impossible for a human being to shrink, yet he continually slipped off Clovis and now he slept in the crook of her arm instead of the other way around as it had been before. Now it must be said that all this appeared to Waldo in the mirror. Except for the fact that he slipped off Clovis and felt smaller than he had before the rest of this information was gathered by looking at himself in the mirror. At first he did not *feel* bad, not bad at all. But he looked terrible.

The awful part was when he finished making love to Clovis for perhaps the tenth or fifteenth time that day he slumped down, stunted and shriveled, knowing full well that he looked dwarfish and ugly. He felt like Wally Dagel. Later he felt scabby. He felt like hell. He even apologized to Clovis for his condition. She said it didn't matter much as long as she got her just do. But Clovis had to admit that Waldo looked pretty scruffy.

What bothered Waldo most was that he had finally decided that Clovis was much older than thirty-seven and that she wasn't so red-hot looking. Sometimes she smelled gamey and her flesh jiggled like the skin of a jelly monster that dies in the invasion-from-outer-space films — the monster that is flanked by algae and the scientist's beautiful daughter — the ripply tattered skin of the monster as he dies with a piteous glug and sags to the floor. She was fleshy and uncorseted and she never closed her mouth or even shaped it when she kissed him. She just sponged the kisses all over his withering body. Suddenly it wasn't as terrific as screwing was usually cracked up to be. He had thought that his mind was changed for good. Previously he had been wounded when he threw himself on Clovis, as if he had thrown himself to cook in a big oven. Then he rode shotgun, got good at it and even enjoyed it. Now he sized up Clovis and saw an old dying jelly monster and he looked at himself in the mirror and saw a boy molting into a twig. She looked old, he looked terrible.

Waldo thought that something had to be done before it was too late. He had become a brilliant liar (he told Clovis that he molted every year but that it soon went away) and certainly knew the value of a dollar and had learned to report everything he had seen. There was positively no reason why he couldn't go out and earn a living wage on the basis of what Clovis had taught him.

"I'm ready," he said to Clovis one day.

"Are you really?" she said.

Waldo went into the bathroom that held so many memories for him. He avoided looking into the mirror but brushed his teeth and dabbed his crinkly skin with a towel. Then he went to the closet and got his suit ready. The bug-eyed bellhop brought up a clean shirt and a new pair of shoes. Waldo also borrowed a pencil and some paper from him and very soon he was ready. He looked at Clovis. She was lying on the bed in her usual pose, naked (she looked like a very weatherbeaten saddle that had been tossed there).

"I'm ready," he said again.

The first thing that Clovis did was to snap up the shade. It sprung into the roller and Waldo looked out. It was night.

"But even if it was day," Clovis said, "I wouldn't let you go. Come here and give me a big hug and a kiss."

Waldo stood frozen. It was night.

Clovis took hold of his tie and pulled him over to the bed, just the way someone would pull a pet something or other, gently but firmly. She tugged him, but once she started tugging him he came on his own. When Clovis saw that he had given up the idea of going, she said, "Tomorrow we'll see Jasper."

Chapter Sixteen

"You got hustle?"

"He's got hustle."

"I suppose I do."

"You need hustle if you wanna be a reporter. And savvy."

"He's got savvy."

"I'm pretty sure I've got savvy."

"No bull," said Jasper. "I need someone with a little savvy."

"He's got a lot."

"Sure you do," said Jasper. "What happened at college?"

"He didn't like it."

"I didn't like it."

"But you were in the pen."

"For a while."

"He did some writing there."

"A little."

"More than I did. It's a good place, the pen, if you can take all the raunch. Anyone ever tell you that?"

"You did."

"Well, it's true. Or it was in my day."

"What about the job?"

"He said he did some writing. What about that?"

"I did a human interest thing at Booneville."

"You interested in human interest?"

"More or less."

"He is."

"Reason I ask is we got a human interest thing going. I won't say it's not sweaty, but it's as human interest as these things go. You interested?"

"I guess so."

"Can't be choosy in this racket. But you're a lucky fella. I got a coupla sweethearts here. Our rare-disease department."

"Sounds fabulous."

"It's a start. The kid wants a start."

"What do I have to do?"

"Simple. I been letting this one sit, let the mother get up tight about her kid. So she's ready. Seems her kid upped and died from a rare one. Lives in town — the old lady, not the kid, the kid died like I said. Tragic really. It'll be a killer in print. All you have to do is get it down. I give you a tape recorder and you get her talking. It won't be any trouble because she's up tight as it is. We get the stuff off the tape, pose some chimpy pictures of the kid, and you're in."

"That's the human interest angle?"

"Sure. He wants the job, doesn't he?"

"He says he does."

"I do."

"What about the writing angle?"

"What writing angle? Look, this is a newspaper, not a writers' colony."

"You got any other stories?"

"I told you once this one's a sweetheart. Lady named Czap."

"Did you say *Czap?* A lady named Czap?"

"I think that's what he said."

"Kid had the crud or something. And boy is she up tight!"

"Grammy sort of went to his funeral. She picked dandelions in the cemetery and happened to be there."

"Saleswise it's our best story."

"Grammy died of old age."

"So did the kid! So did the kid! Only the kid was about ten years old! How about that? I told you it's a honey, didn't I? It'll be murder in print."

"That day the dogs peed on Grammy's dandelions. She wouldn't have picked them only they kept her afloat during the depression."

"Did you say the kid died of old age at *ten?*"

"I told you once. A skin disease, I think. The crud. There's a fortune to be made in rare diseases. We're just starting to scratch the surface, too. They sort of grow on you."

"If he knows the lady there won't be any problem."

"A fortune. If he can handle it."

"I was hoping there'd be some writing involved."

"Forget it. If you've got hustle you don't have to worry about writing."

"He's been counting on this. He's been on the edge of his seat waiting to be a reporter — that's all he's talked about for weeks!"

"That right?"

"Well, not the edge of my seat. But I want to be a reporter very much."

"*Very* much. I couldn't get a word in edgewise!"

"Way I see it, you look like you got hustle. Look a little pale, though."

"He's *molting,* he said. Isn't he a card!"

"Sure is."

"It's funny how I know that lady Czap. I hope she remembers who I am."

"I think she will."

"Doesn't matter. It's the kid we're worried about. With the crud. If Waldo gets in there and gets a few hunnert feet of tape off her he's got it licked."

Chapter Seventeen

"There's one thing I want to make clear right off — my baby, Willy, was perfectly normal the day he was born. He probably caught the thing at school or something. When we found out that he had it, it was too late," said Mrs. Czap recrossing her legs a third time.

Waldo adjusted the tape recorder. "How do you spell it?"

"Dunno. There's a jerry in it."

"Louder please," Waldo urged.

"I said, *there's a jerry in it!*" Mrs. Czap then put her head very close to the tape recorder and spoke to the machine, trying to reason with it. "I hope you understand that stuff like that is very hard to spell." She got up and went to a stack of newspapers near a telephone. ". . . thought I wrote it here someplace when the doctor . . . *here it is!*" She tore off a corner of one of the newspapers and waved it at Waldo. "I *knew* it was here someplace," she exclaimed smiling triumphantly at the ragged bit of newsprint.

The woman then seated herself across from Waldo once again and placed the paper very carefully on the table. She put her head close to it and grimaced at it for a while. "Trying to read my writing," she muttered without looking up at Waldo.

"Here, let me look," said Waldo, reaching for the scrap of paper.

The woman snatched it off the table and held it back, away

from Waldo. "Wait a minute, will you?" Waldo turned down the tape recorder. "I think I can read *my own hand-writing* a little bit better than you!"

Waldo apologized, then turned up the tape recorder.

Mrs. Czap looked at the piece of paper. She closed one eye and then the other. She fished for a food particle in one of her back teeth with her tongue. Finally, she swallowed, straightened her back, and spelled the name of the rare disease into the microphone. She looked at the machine as if it were going to speak back to her, perhaps tell her not to worry any more, Willy was in good hands. The spools of the machine continued to revolve with almost no noise.

Waldo turned to the machine. "That would be *progeria*."

The machine said nothing. But it listened very closely to what was being said. It was like a very wise and silent third person in the room with them. Both Waldo and Mrs. Czap were apprehensive about it.

"It was awful," said the woman.

"Into the microphone, please," said Waldo.

"It was *awful*," the woman repeated bending toward the machine.

The woman shifted on the chair and looked at Waldo slowly like a range finder. Then her lips pursed in remorse and she stared at the bridge of Waldo's nose. Waldo leaned on the table toward her and patted the slim bones on the top of her otherwise fat hands. The woman merely unclenched her fist when Waldo did this and let her hand fall limp against the plastic of the tablecloth.

Waldo listened to the hum of the refrigerator for a while and seeing the silent woman said, "It must have been awful."

"Oh, it *was* — I wanna tell you," the woman said. "I mean you know how old men are — real *old* men? If you've ever lived under the same roof with an old man, then I won't have to tell you what a trial Willy was."

"Yes. Into the microphone, please," said Waldo.

". . . not that we minded him bothering and whining about everything. I mean, *Willy had an incurable disease.*"

The woman's forehead wrinkled. She is raising her eyebrows, thought Waldo, although they've all been plucked out. The woman finished with, "I wanna tell you."

"Yes," said Waldo into the microphone, "he had an incurable disease."

"Well, we didn't mind all the trouble and stuff. But he did seem to have," the woman was speaking in her throat, "he *did* seem to have more than the usual . . . ah . . . you know."

"The usual . . ."

"The usual . . . *complaints,* I guess you'd call them; like 'the TV is too loud' or he'd lisp on purpose because he knew I hated lisping. Or he'd fight us — we were careful never to hurt him — we knew he was sick. Sometimes, though, he'd talk about bowel movements all day and never do anything helpful. Well, it was always something, I'm telling you. But poor little Willy. Went ahead and died just the same. *Horible* business."

"Bowel movements all day," Waldo repeated into the microphone.

"Oh, we couldn't blame *him*," the woman keened, throwing her head to the side and fixing her eyes on a plaster of Paris Christ statue that had been made into a bank that stood, bleeding and merciful on the refrigerator along with a dish of stale bread.

"Wasn't his fault," said Waldo with some conviction.

"Certainly *not*," the woman said, her voice rising and falling as if in song. "The doctor told me that anyone, *anyone* can get it, really. Everybody, if you can imagine that. Mostly kids get it though."

"I see," said Waldo.

"Now, don't get the idea that I gave it to him." The woman held the microphone in her hand and looked at it. "You don't think that *I* gave it to him, do you? Well, *do you?*"

"No," said Waldo, "I don't."

But the woman did not look at Waldo. She continued to look at the microphone, she continued to explain to the machine. "Someone accused *me* of giving it to him. Why . . . it's downright foolish, that's what it is. It's silly to think that I could give him a horrible thing like that. I told you it was *incurable*. I couldn't give him something *incurable*, could I?"

"I don't think it's possible."

"It wasn't like I took an airplane ride when I was pregnant or even rode the bus much, let alone go and get drunk and fall downstairs like *some neighbors I know*." The woman said the last phrase too loud, as if someone were at her window outside, listening. "To tell you the honest truth, I never been in a plane," she continued sullenly, "and at this rate I prolly never will. When I was carrying Willy I cut down to a pack a day. No real drinking. A short beer now and then — I hardly drink anyways, so it doesn't matter, I suppose."

Waldo poised himself for a question, but the woman murmured on, barely moving her lips and still talking hoarsely, down in her throat. "Everyone said I was the picture of health. The *picture of health*. It was a good pregnancy — everyone said so. My sister-in-law came in on Fridays to get the house picked up. I quit my job at the electronics plant . . ."

Waldo fiddled with the knobs of the tape recorder and tried to think of a good question to ask Mrs. Czap. But he could think of nothing.

". . . so the doctor was real happy with my progress. I was feeling fine and I didn't have any whuddayacallits . . . ah . . . discharges, at all. Like I say, everyone said I was the picture of health."

Both were silent for a while. Mrs. Czap looked around the room rather furtively, as if looking for her lost momentum. Waldo began to speak, but he was interrupted by the woman, and when they were both speaking at once Waldo saw that she had no intention of stopping. Waldo clicked his retractable pen in protest and let the woman continue into the microphone.

"And after a year," she was saying, "he showed signs of being a pretty good-looking kid. No Ronald Fairbanks or anything like that, you understand, but . . . not a *bad-looking kid*. Had his old man's — " The woman mumbled a prayer. " — eyes and nose. My mouth. That's all he had of ours, though."

"Do you have any pictures of him?"

"Of who?"

"Of Willy."

"No. Unless you count pictures he sneaked into. He used to run up and stick his head in pictures at the last minute. Drove everyone crazy. I think the doctor took his pictures and they took them at school, for the records."

"Willy went to school?"

"Sure he did. Got good grades too. We promised him a present if he brought home a good report card. So when he got all A's we bought him a turtle in a plastic bowl. He really liked that little green thing. We couldn't have bought him a better prize — only two bits for the turtle, fifty for the bowl. It was plastic and had a special ramp for the turtle to walk on."

"Willy liked the turtle," Waldo said in the direction of the microphone.

"*Liked* the turtle! He *loved* the thing. He stared at it all day Saturday when the other kids went to the show. And instead of watching television he watched *it*. Willy and that little turtle were the best of friends . . . I could hear them talking from the kitchen. It was great while it lasted — you can't imagine what it did for Willy." She paused. "But, easy come, easy go."

Waldo said yes a little uncertainly.

"You know how it is," the woman said. "Nothing really lasts long, does it?"

"I'll say not," said Waldo sincerely.

"We just came in one morning and there he was."

"A little louder please," said Waldo detecting the crucial note in Mrs. Czap's voice.

"There he was. We were all sad. The oldest boy screamed and yelled and threw himself on the floor and even tore his shirt off. Course we wouldn't have done it all if it wasn't for Willy. We figured we owed it to the poor little kid."

"He was your son."

"You'll never know the heartbreak of it all."

"I remember Grammy telling me," said Waldo.

"But that wasn't all of it. Not by a long shot. We got a regular little casket for him and even tiny little flowers and like that. What I mean is, everything was the same except smaller. As small as we could get it, really." Waldo looked up and when his eyes met those of the woman he looked down again. "What I mean is we gave the little guy a regular little funeral with candles and all. And people sent stuff . . ."

"Everyone knew Willy," said Waldo trying to think if he had ever seen him around the neighborhood.

"*I'll say* they all knew Willy," the woman said. "Why, I'm telling you when it came to cookies and milk he *cleaned* up. They all adored him. I mean," she nodded, "*adored* him."

"So, naturally they all came to the funeral."

"Sure, why not? They figured it'd only be an hour or so. It was for Willy, they figured."

"Of course. And for you too, Mrs. Czap."

"Oh, they prolly figured it would help us out of a spot."

"A spot?"

"Well, I'm not saying that Willy was *unpopular* — I told you about the cookies and milk — but, after all, there was only this street. That's not many people when you think about it. So, there wasn't enough for a real funeral unless almost everybody came."

"No," said Waldo.

"No," said the woman.

"Must have been terrible."

"Horrible."

"Awful."

"I'm telling you."

"But," said Waldo, "can you give us a few more *de*tails of the . . . funeral."

"I told you about the casket and the little flower things. Did I tell you about the candles? *They* were *dar*ling — the kind you put on a birthday cake."

"Birthday candles?"

"Those are the only ones we figured would be small enough."

"Yes. They *are* small," Waldo said scratching his head. "Was there anything else you think we should know?"

"No. Other than that it was just about like every other turtle funeral. Every other *two-bit* turtle funeral. They must have big ones in the zoos where they have those big turtles that lay the eggs. You didn't see that movie by any chance?"

"*Turtle funeral?*" Waldo said, furrowing his forehead into thousands of little frowns. "Did you say *turtle funeral?*"

"Well . . . *yes.* I toldja the turtle only cost a quarter. And fifty for the bowl. I wasn't lying. Honest."

"I believe you," Waldo said.

The woman was silent. She had lost her momentum once again. But instead of allowing herself to be interrupted she began mumbling to herself. Soon he caught phrases he could understand. Waldo aimed the machine at her and it was not long before Mrs. Czap was speaking audibly at a good rate.

". . . or maybe it was the wrong kind of water or food, or maybe it was the air — lousy — too hot or too cold. Or the bowl . . . *it* might have been wrong, although it had a ramp and was real nice plastic and cost fifty cents. I don't know. Maybe he picked him up too much, you know, *handled* him . . . or maybe not enough . . ." Her voice trailed off as if her mind were narrowing the way her eyes were. She said, "I don't know" again.

"Willy was attached to that turtle. Do you have a picture of the tur . . ."

". . . anyway, he got soft. His shell. Although it wasn't colored like most two-bit turtles . . . and he died."

". . . maybe Willy posing with the turtle . . ."

"We wanted to buy him another one. It's only a quarter turtle, I said to him. But he only wanted that old soft turtle with the green shell. Green shells are hard to get — mostly they have colors or flowers on them. And Willy's turtle was squishy and smelled and I couldn't look at it after he dug it up — it got pieces of lint on it from being carried around in his pocket. Pretty soon it wasn't a turtle at all but a linty old ball of dead." The woman's voice droned into the machine. It sounded as if she were speaking through a network of rubber bands.

"So I guess I'll check the school for pictures," Waldo said.

"I used to hear him cry sometimes at night, Willy."

There was silence in the room for a long time. Even the woman's last word, the name, was gone. The sun going down illuminated the tops of things: the broken lamp on the table, the head of the woman, Mrs. Czap, her hair in wild Gorgon strands stuck out, made gold by the late afternoon sun. The plaster Christ pocked under the beams and the bread was lost in the shadow of the bank.

"Then he got old, from the disease."

"Incurable," said Waldo into the microphone.

"And after his hair turned white he started to go bald. He got tired by just walking to the neighbors for milk . . . and he stopped talking even after I told him I loved him and would do anything in the world for him. Anything at all — if he'd just name it. I was pregnant again and he used to watch me and not say anything. Used to watch everybody and wait."

"Used to wait," Waldo repeated.

"He waited in the corner there and just let all his hair fall out and his teeth, too . . ."

"Fell out," said Waldo.

". . . skin got all white and wrinkly and I was sick every morning and sleeping in the afternoon, although my sister-in-law came in again to help me. But it *wasn't the same* — even though I let him use the playpen we bought for the new baby. He was small, Willy, and he seemed to be shrinking. I *told him* I loved him. Believe me, I told him all the time. *All the time.*"

"Of course," Waldo said.

"He used to watch me from the playpen — from be-tween the bars. I remember doing things in the kitchen and having to look at him all the time . . . skin all wrinkly like grass . . . Finally, I had to move him out of the kitchen and into the hall because I couldn't do anything while he was looking at me. His hands were on arms — thin like sticks — with lips, blue, and almost no face because it got hollow and he could look through the bars easy at me, but there wasn't any place I could move him. I just had to look. And he sort of hunched over and peeked his head through the bars . . ."

Waldo moved in his chair.

". . . just looked out from the bars like he wanted me to tell him that I made him like that, which wasn't true because I told you myself I loved him and I did. I couldn't come right out and say, *I didn't do it to you, Willy* because he never said anything — just looked at me with his old body and his little hands with long fingernails around the bars of the play- pen . . ."

"That disease," Waldo said. "Horrible."

"It was him. And it got so . . . I couldn't even . . ." The woman gasped once. Then she said, "look." She sobbed dryly, still gasping, then shut her mouth tight and left Waldo and the microphone and looked at the sun for a long while.

"My feet swelled up," Mrs. Czap said at last. "And so did my legs. Pretty soon I knew it was going to come any day." She paused. "The night I had the baby . . ." She stopped, then picked up again. "The night I had the baby Willy didn't sleep in the playpen like usual. He went for a walk — even though we told him never go out of the house. He walked all the way outside of town where the big trees are . . . the ones on the calendars."

Waldo could not think of the name of the big trees.

"And that's where they found him next morning. All curled up and lying at the foot of the big trees. They took a picture of him lying there with a blanket over him . . ."

"It must have been a very rare disease," Waldo said just remembering that a reporter has to have a lot of hustle and a lot of savvy.

". . . and I was in the hospital with the baby three more days and on the fourth *it* died from something. I was still getting sick every morning. But pretty soon I stopped. Like before."

Waldo saw that the woman had stopped for good. He bent down and switched off the tape recorder. He said, "That story has a lot of human interest. It's very moving and sales-wise at least, very interesting . . ."

But the woman was not listening to him. She was staring at him, her mouth agape, her features carved and distorted. First she looked at his head — the motley patches where Waldo's hair had begun to fall out. Then she looked at the scurf-covered hand that had just switched off the tape recorder. She snatched at his arm. Waldo drew away. She snatched again, caught him and put her face right up close to his as she had done with the piece of paper with Willy's disease written on it.

"Willy?" Mrs. Czap suddenly had a very tiny voice.

Waldo said, "We'll send you a check in tomorrow's mail." Mrs. Czap did not respond to the money. She said the name again and clutched Waldo even tighter.

Then a funny thing happened. It was as if someone had scratched a match inside Waldo's belly. Waldo knew the feeling. He looked at Mrs. Czap. The hands in Waldo's head were bundling up the tape recorder, wrapping the cords and sorting out the plugs. But the hands on the ends of Waldo's arms were patting Mrs. Czap's fleshy thighs. Mrs. Czap loosened and she started to go limp. Waldo felt powerful, he felt he could actually *do* something for this woman. He put his hand under her dress. Mrs. Czap put her arms around Waldo and squeezed him.

"Willy," she said.

What am I doing? Waldo thought. Waldo had trouble controlling himself. The match was still burning, edging its way to the fingers that were holding it under a bunch of his glands.

"We'll go piggyback," said Mrs. Czap. "You always liked piggyback rides."

She doesn't want the money. The death of Willy has affected her good sense. She's crazy. "I'll give you a tip if you let me go," said Waldo. "A fin if you stop squeezing me like that."

Money was no object. Mrs. Czap held on and Waldo couldn't budge her. He had made up his mind that he would do nothing. What right had this woman to make advances? He ignored Mrs. Czap's rude suggestions and cheap tricks and tore himself away.

"Please!" said Mrs. Czap smoothing her dress. "Willy!"

"You're going to make a bundle on this story," said Waldo. "You want the world?"

A fine thing, Waldo thought. I shouldn't have led her on. Shouldn't have teased her. But what right does a woman her age have to try that hanky-panky with me?

Waldo picked up his tape recorder and, feeling very noble and clean, went directly to Jasper's office. *Dying Mother Tells All* appeared in the morning edition.

Chapter Eighteen

Time passed. And one day Waldo went home to visit his mother. From the first moment he laid eyes on her he knew she was suffering from a case of the uglies. He could tell because she pretended not to notice him when he came in. She was busily watering some plastic flowers that were in the window box where the geraniums had been. She hummed to herself and turned her back on Waldo, then she put some old newspapers in order, dusted the coffee table, and, her one good eye fixed straight ahead, walked directly past Waldo to a wastebasket which she emptied out the window (she would not have done this ordinarily except that she knew there was nothing in it so it didn't matter whether she emptied it out the window or not). As soon as Waldo seated himself on the sofa she came over and motioned for him to get up. Waldo stood. His mother plumped the cushions vigorously, kept plumping and looking at Waldo who was in back of her. With her left eye naturally turned out and her good eye turned in exactly the opposite direction she appeared to have two wall-eyes. Waldo looked around one side and saw a green eye looking at him; he peeked around the other side and saw the blue one looking at him. It gave him the creeps. He went to the other side of the room and sat down.

Waldo's mother marched across the room and tripped over Waldo's stretched-out legs.

"Will you watch what you're doing!" she screamed.

"Ma?" Waldo said softly.

"What do you want?" Waldo was right. She *did* have the uglies. Waldo felt like leaving.

"I'm back."

"I see you."

"You do?"

"I asked you once, what do you want?" Waldo's mother trembled, all the gruesome little complaints curdled in her voice as she spoke.

"Do I have to want something to come home?"

"Other people don't. You do. Now tell me and make it snappy. I haven't got time to talk. You can see how busy I am. What's that stuff on your skin and for goodness sake what happened to your hair?"

"Nothing."

"Nothing? Look at your hair, Waldo. Look at your hair and tell me that's nothing."

"I've seen it. It's nothing."

"Is it one of those fancy haircuts?"

"No."

"Is it some kind of disease?"

"No."

"Well, I don't like the looks of that hair one bit. If you think you're going to waltz in this house with hair like that you've got another think coming. I won't allow it."

"I can't help it. It just got that way."

"Don't come in here and tell me you can't help it. I've got enough to worry about without worrying about your hair — God knows where you've been for the past six months, I suppose that's none of my business, I can't go around watching over you like a mother. But I've had it up to here." She put her left hand at about the level of her mad eye to indicate that she was fed up. "The dryer's on the fritz again. I suppose you don't care about that either."

"The what?"

"The dryer."

"What does it dry?"

"Dishes. You know it dries dishes. Are you trying to egg me on, Waldo?"

"You want it fixed? I'll get it fixed." Waldo took some money out of his pocket and offered it to his mother.

"What is that, Waldo? May I ask?"

"It's money."

"I didn't ask you what it is. I know it's money — what do you think I am? I asked you what it's for — listen to me when I talk to you. You never listen."

"It's to fix your dish dryer."

"Keep it."

"I don't need a dish dryer."

"Keep your money! Keep it! I'm sure you need it more than we do."

"I don't."

"Keep it anyway. Get your hair fixed. Don't worry about my dryer — your hair is much more important. Oh, I remember what lovely hair you used to have. It was soft and had a lovely sheen. We used to comb it together. The comb never stuck because your hair was never snarly like some people's hair is. And now look at you — you're a mess! I hate hair like that, like you've been plastering it with goo. It's hateful hair and I won't look at it a minute longer. Go away, Waldo, I don't want to look at your hair."

"Don't look, then. You don't *have* to look. I just came home to see how you and Dad are. I've been busy or I would've come sooner."

"It looks doggy, that hair. It looks crumby."

"Will you stop talking about my hair!" Waldo got to his feet and faced his mother. His mother's right eye was staring at his hair.

"It breaks my heart to look at your hair," Waldo's mother said.

"No one's asking you to look. Now will you tell me how you and dad are? Is everything okay?"

"How could you come home looking like that? Are you a beatnik? Is that why your hair looks so funny?"

"It's a very rare disease."

"Well, you may think it's all right to look that way. You don't have to answer to the neighbors. You just come and go like this was a hotel. Is that the *style* nowadays? Is it the style to insult your mother and make your hair awful because you know how much it bothers your mother to have it that way? I wish your father were here — he'd tell you, Waldo, you look queer as an ash barrel!"

"I bought him a new truss," said Waldo, fidgeting with a large box and pulling out something that looked like a rucksack from a nest of tissue paper.

"We don't want your filthy presents. Why don't you just take it back where you got it? Why don't you go!"

Waldo started to back up. He said nothing for a moment or two and then he said, very quietly, "Look, if I do — if I *do* go away — I'll never set foot in this house again, I'll never listen to one more word from you and I won't give a good god-damn if you and dad drop dead and don't have a single daisy on your grave!"

Waldo saw that his mother's face swelled with rage when he said that he'd never set foot in the house, but her face became tiny and white when Waldo talked about dropping dead. The explosion that could have followed such an outburst would have made it any man's ball game. And so, seeing that his mother had possession of the rucksack and might decide to bean him with it, or something worse, he added, "That's *if* I go and maybe I won't . . ."

It was quite a while, maybe five minutes, before Waldo's mother could speak. When she did she spoke quietly, wetting her lips as she spoke. "No one would believe this, Waldo, not a soul. I wish someone were here to listen to you talking to me that way. No one would believe you are my son, no one would believe my only son would treat me this way. Look at the treatment I get! Look at it! Why, if someone were here listening they'd make a movie and I'd bet they'd make a pretty penny on it, too. All that time you were gone I began to believe that I loved you and now I know I was crazy to think I could do such a thing. If you only knew me, Waldo, if you only loved me, you'd know how much I hate you. And I can't cry any more about that because I'm all cried out."

"Well, for crying out loud, all that talk about hair makes me mad."

"*You* don't have to look at your hair! *You* can't see it — it's on your head! But I can see it and I can tell you honest and truly it looks terrible!"

"I told you six times *don't look!*"

"All right, I won't," Waldo's mother said curtly and with that she picked up a cushion, went behind the sofa and lay down, out of sight.

"What are you doing?"

The voice was muffled. It said: "I can't talk to you if I have to look at your disgusting hair. Please sit down, Waldo. If you want to talk we can talk — it'll be like talking on the phone. Fun. You never called up once and told us anything . . ." The voice stopped.

Waldo looked at his mother — or at as much of his mother as he could see. There was the sofa, battered, with the springs protruding from the cushions and other slighter stony bulges. It too looked like Clovis's jelly-monster, fleshy, bulgy. But it was so big that soon Waldo imagined that it was an old headless animal with short legs. And this fat frayed beast was squatting on his mother whose feet protruded and showed her to be cold and dumb. Indeed, those gnarled silent feet were all that remained of his mother. Waldo sat down in a chair opposite the squatting sofa. He lit a cigarette and waited for a voice.

He heard the hucking of phlegm and then, "Waldo, is that *you?*" His mother actually spoke as if she were talking on the telephone.

"Yes."

"You okay?"

"Yes."

"No ills?"

"No."

"Good."

"You?"

"We're all fine here. Tip-top."

"Good."

There was a pause, a buzz in Waldo's ears.

"Waldo?"

"Yes?"

"May I ask you a teensy question?"

"Yes."

"How could you do it to us?"

"Uh?"

"I said, *how could you do it to us?*"

"Do what? The hair?"

"Do you know what they're doing for that woman?"

"What woman?"

"Do you have any idea of the amount of money that has been sent to Sybil Czap? Have you any inkling?"

"She got hers. I haven't been keeping up. Been busy."

"*Thousands!* Thousands and thousands of dollars have

been sent in from all over the country. The woman is *drowning* in money and it's your doing, Waldo, it's all your doing."

Waldo raised an eyebrow at his mother's feet and said, "I'm a reporter — that's my job. It wasn't easy to get the job, but I got it and I try to tell it like it is. If Czap got a few extra shells for blowing the whistle on her kid that's her orange juice. I can't help it. It's my job."

"I suppose you know they wrote a song about Willy — *The Ballad of Willy Czap*." There was a distinct sob from behind the sofa. "It's on the Hit Parade!"

"Yeah, I heard it — catchy little tune, eh?" Waldo dum-de-dummed his way through the first few bars of *The Ballad of Willy Czap*.

"And that's not all. Sybil Czap has been given luggage, a new car, parakeets, and they even gave her her own personal crater on the moon, named after Willy! Can you *imagine? . . .*"

"*Who* gave that woman a crater?"

". . . her name is a household word! That little beast used to come over here begging for a glass of milk. And I was stupid enough to give it to him. It's probably *my* fault he lived so long!"

Waldo's mother's feet drummed up and down as if she was trapped under the sofa and struggling to get free. Each time she spoke she thumped her feet on the floor, she cursed and apparently was banging her head as well because each foot-thump was accompanied by another thump, muffled, from the hidden end of his mother. She went on and on, enumerating Sybil Czap's many prizes and great good luck in having an ordinary son with a rare disease. Sybil had had her hair done, her face lifted, and had been deluged with money and marriage proposals — men from all over the world sought the hand that patted the prematurely grizzled head of Willy.

"You've ruined us, Waldo!" She screamed. "We're ruined for *life* and it's all your doing. They've turned her house into a museum and set up booths outside selling Willy Czap sweatshirts. Why, everything that little boy *touched* is worth a mint!"

"So she got a little dough. So what? You haven't given me any good reasons why you should go off your head about this . . ."

"*Reasons!* Don't talk to me about reasons, Waldo. I'm your mother — have you forgotten that? Reasons! Why your father works and slaves like a dog to keep us in good healthy food. I do my best. And *you* — you turn around and slap us in the face. That's the last straw! I don't have to take any more from you. I don't have to if I don't want to. Who ever said kids are grateful? I'd like to know. I'd kill him with my bare hands! Grateful? My eye! You spit at us and then run us into the ground. I hate you for this, I *know* I do, God forgive me for what I'm saying. Your father went out looking for you — he's been looking for you ever since they set up those booths in front of the Czap house. If he finds you he's going to whip the tar out of you!"

Two hands became visible above the sofa and clenched themselves into little nut-like fists and banged together in remorse, then fell out of sight. "First you make our lives miserable at home and have to be sent to jail, then you worry us half to death by running off to that school and don't call. Oh, that's all right. Sure, that's fine. Then we come up and *tell* you in plain English . . ." There was a sigh from the I-don't-know-why-I'm-bothering-to-tell-you school of badgering and then his mother continued slowly. ". . . we say to you very, very plain and simple that Grammy has passed on, died, and that there isn't the slightest chance she'll ever come back . . ."

Waldo listened closely when the name of Grammy was mentioned. He had not thought about her for a long time. He had even stopped mentioning her to Clovis who had grown tired of hearing about the old bird. But Grammy would have been the only one who could have walked in there and shut her daughter up properly. And now she was dead, Grammy.

"And you do this to us!" More sighs and groans. "I can't take it, I can't. Sybil Czap is Mother of the Year. She has everything and we could have had every bit of it . . ."

"Sometimes I miss Grammy," said Waldo. "She always said that we'd miss her and I never believed her — but I do miss her off and on. I think about her there in the cemetery digging up weeds to eat."

"So you *think* about her! That's big of you, mighty big! But what do you go and do? You go and write about Sybil Czap and don't give a hoot about your family. No. You never did and you never will because it's too late now. These things are only good once. If you were to write about a dead lady now they'd all think we were after the money."

"Which money?"

"Sure you think about Grammy, sure you do. The next thing you'll tell me is that you loved her very much."

"I did — I'm pretty sure I did."

"That's a lie."

"It's not a lie. I loved her."

"It's a lie. You weren't even listening when we told you she was dead and would never come back. You couldn't have been or you wouldn't have done what you did. You would have taken some pity on her, on us, maybe. Maybe on us who love you! Instead you go and take a perfect stranger, Sybil Czap, who never gave you a second look. I'm not complaining, Waldo. I'm just saying that you can't go around telling people that I'm your mother and that you loved Grammy when you didn't have the common decency to write your story about Grammy's death."

"I never thought of it, come to think of it."

"Because you're rotten to the core, that's why."

Waldo wasn't really sure whether he hadn't written about Grammy because he loved her or because there was no money in it. Lots of other people had written about the dear dead days passed in their Grammy's stuffy, gingerbread-smelling parlors. The lovable shrunken Grammys. If he had loved her, he thought, what good would it do to talk about it? It's the stuff you don't know anything about, the stuff that scares you and you're on the verge of hating you've got to write about, Waldo thought, sweaty stories, nightmares or not. Those are the ones that keep you awake, he thought, and he was sure that there was no sense and very little money in the other kind. But how do you go about explaining this to your mother?

"I loved her," said Waldo.

"Don't talk to me about love, Waldo. You're rotten right clean through! You know I could've told you the story of how she died of old age. I could have done it better than that Sybil Czap who doesn't appreciate what the American people have done for her. I'm a dying mother — don't you think I'm dying enough to tell you about Grammy? Don't you think I'm dying enough to win a free trip to California or get a marriage proposal? You can keep talking and keep explaining but someday you'll realize that you let us down. Look what you've done to me, Waldo! Look what you've made me!"

Waldo saw the two feet slide into the sofa and as that was happening his mother's head poked up from the back. The sofa-monster now had a head.

"Look what you've done to me! You big shot, wise guy,

blowhard — are you happy? Look at me, you son of a bitch!"

His mother's face looked lustful — the way Mrs. Czap's face had looked when she put her arms around Waldo and squeezed him and wouldn't let go. There were sleazy pockets in her cheeks and frowzy lines around her eyes; her hair was frizzed in all directions. Mrs. Czap had no right to make those advances on Waldo. She had no intention of paying him, not the slightest. She only wanted a little free fun. But this greedy face staring over the top of the sofa — that was his mother, she was entitled to it free of charge. Waldo was frightened. He knew what was coming. She would start that why-did-you-do-it-to-us business all over again and then expect Waldo to climb all over her. No, he was a one-woman man and he could not betray Clovis.

"I'm sick of it," said Waldo's mother. "I can't do it any longer. I don't want to be your mother any more — there are too many heartaches and setbacks. I just look at your hair and I get sick, and then I think of what you did to us and how you forgot Grammy that way and I want to kill you. I can't go on like this — you're no use to us any more. I'm through."

Good, thought Waldo, she doesn't want to be my mother. That means she's not entitled to anything free. Yes, she looks very hungry, but that doesn't give her any rights.

Waldo got up. His mother stared at his hair and almost smiled, as if someday she would get her chance to tell about how he had died. After a decent period of time elapsed, after people forgot about Sybil Czap and Willy, Waldo's mother would tell about him and get rich. So that's how it is, Waldo thought. He went directly outside and scrambled into Clovis's Cadillac and took off like a shot. It was late and Clovis had not had her just do. There was no need ever to come back home again.

Chapter Nineteen

But Mrs. Czap was not the only one that profited from the
interview in Jasper's newspaper. If Mrs. Czap made a few
extra shells on the thing, Jasper and Waldo made a bundle.
Mrs. Czap had become the exclusive property of Jasper and
Jasper wouldn't let anyone look at her until a contract was
drawn up stating clearly the number of looks, blinks and
ganders the person would take — at so much per look. Jasper
also engineered the sweatshirt contract and set up the booths
that disturbed Waldo's father.

Waldo was hailed as a blazing new talent, full of wit and
verve, with a sharp ear for dialogue and a sharp eye for human interest. He was someone to be watched, fresh, vivid,
uproarious, original, marvelous, with real fire, brilliance, and
with heart-stopping moments of disturbing insight. He made
people howl with laughter and bang on the walls with grief.
His deft pen had turned the story of Mrs. Czap and her late
son into a wildly gruesome, dazzling, bitterly savage, funny
rollicking, Joycean parable, a triumph with classical rhythms,
a masterpiece, Greek in implication, unsurpassed in high
comedy, Whitmanesque in conception, containing unforget-
table moments in the Menagerie we call Life Itself. Waldo
was well on his way to becoming nothing less than the most
gifted writer of ripe mid-century Americana. His reportage
was flawless, his genius keen and sure and fine, and he had
succeeded in getting down on paper and ordering between

covers the only non-fiction surrealistic story ever written.

Whenever she read these reviews in the papers Clovis said the same thing: "It's enough to give you a shit-fit!" She felt threatened by the praise and made Waldo promise that he would never leave her, not for a minute. She had made him what he was, she said, and he couldn't bite the hand that was feeding him just because it was the closest one to his mouth.

So they were four: Waldo, Clovis, Jasper and Mrs. Czap. Jasper bought a bus and they planned a tour together. This arrangement pleased Mrs. Czap who was still convinced that Waldo was really her little boy Willy who had somehow faked a disappearance, grown a foot and, according to the critics, acquired a way with words. They would travel throughout the country giving lectures and demonstrations. The high point of the evening would come when Waldo and Mrs. Czap would seat themselves before thousands of people and repeat the famous Dying-Mother-Tells-All-About Dead-Son interview. This time Waldo would be madly scribbling away on a notepad while Mrs. Czap moved her lips in time with the tape recorder spinning out the story of Willy's death.

Jasper was disappointed at not being able to play the part of the roving reporter. But his prison record — the unfortunate incident with those little girls and that major swindle — was well-known. Certainly better known than Waldo's own felonious assault on the truss. People would be suspicious.

Clovis was delighted with Mrs. Czap. She had Mrs. Czap tell the story of Willy many times and took a sheer innocent joy in paying Mrs. Czap each time, as she had done with Waldo. She was responsible for the story improving considerably — many details were added by Mrs. Czap to please Clovis. The four sat around the hotel room until late in the evening. Mrs. Czap was the prima donna most of the time. She told the story in several different versions, then got busy with her daily syndicated column of medical advice to mothers. Jasper, Clovis and Waldo read the letters aloud and Mrs. Czap dictated replies to the tape recorder. Mrs. Czap offered home remedies for everything and insisted that it was tender loving care that accounted for most recoveries. She usually started each reply by saying, "There's one thing I want to get straight right off . . ."

Waldo's condition had not improved. He was taken to many skin specialists and none of them could diagnose his affliction. Finally he had to settle for weekly visits to a doctor who smoothed his skin down with a high-pressure air hose. After each treatment he had rosy cheeks and a happy glow about him which lasted for several days. It was only on the day of the visit that the decay became apparent and this was quickly whisked off. Clovis's pride and joy was the wig she had made for Waldo. Each hair was flown in from a chilly northern country where the people are lovely and blond and romp all day long in the sun. Each hair was stuck carefully into the headpiece and finally Waldo was crowned with it.

Clovis said over and over again that those were the happiest days of her life, rivaled only by the days she had spent traveling with the theater troupe. But the theater days had been so pansified and soiled by the leading men that she really couldn't compare them. She now took simple pleasure in staying in the background. In newspaper articles on Waldo she was sometimes referred to as Waldo's "constant companion." But that's as far as it went. No one ever made any unkind references to her. People understood completely the quirks that writers have and how sensitive they are about their personal lives. The public could see that Waldo had a talent to reckon with, so they left Clovis alone for the most part.

Waldo took it all in stride. Clovis had been (and still was) kind to him. She was a generous and thoughtful person and one fine day she would die. On that day Waldo would begin her story, just as John had begun the Gladys story, Morris the grandmother story, Mrs. Czap the Willy story, just as his mother would spill the beans about his skin disease and dead hair; indeed, just as all the bereaved flung themselves at typewriters as soon as the last scoopful of dirt was chucked at the foot of the gravestone. You couldn't blame them for it.

It was strange how people now took on a whole new aspect. They *were* important after all. And not just the Johns and Morrises and Mrs. Czaps. No, each single person had a story and those stories were worth money. Everyone — even the lowest on earth — had resale value. The ones like Clovis were worth the most money. They had been places, their stories were colorful and outrageous. Of course if they told the stories they would become household words. If someone else told the story they could share the fame. And if they were dead, like Gladys, the biographer would get the reward — even if it was the dubious reward of holding forth in a pay toilet, like John. Clovis was perfect. She had been a starlet and Waldo knew her intimately. Waldo spent long hours thinking along these lines.

Waldo wasn't the only one in the quartet with terrific ideas. Jasper had a few of his own. Jasper's best was the glass writer's-cage that he had built for Waldo. He explained that Waldo would get in and then, in someplace like the Mandrake Club, Waldo could demonstrate just how it was done, writing, a writer writing. It would be murder. And it would also take up where Mrs. Czap left off. Next year another

Mother of the Year would be elected, or maybe Mrs. Czap would welch on her contract and marry one of the pen pals she had acquired. In that case Waldo's writing act would be a natural.

Clovis thought that it was a cute idea. She added that Waldo was at liberty to do whatever he pleased as long as she got what was coming to her. She wouldn't push Waldo into anything, certainly not into a glass writing-cage if he didn't want to go. But it was a catchy little idea. He could try it and if he didn't like it he wouldn't have to stay. In the meantime she wanted nothing more than her just do. That shouldn't be much of a chore. People in love were like those snakes in fat skins that gobble themselves into a sheath and an ever-tightening circle. But Clovis would never ask too much as long as Waldo learned the simple rules of give and take.

So anyway, about a year after Waldo's release from Booneville Jasper landed a contract for Waldo and Mrs. Czap at the Mandrake Club. They were all very excited about it and Mrs. Czap kept saying that she was all nerved up because of the la-dee-dah; who would believe it and so on. It was decided that she should rehearse her heartbreaking story just in case anything went wrong with the tape recorder. Nothing could be left to chance. She did this gladly and with a tight corset on. The corset made her voice change if it was drawn very tight. She really sounded heartbroken; the remorse strained against the corset, she breathed heavily, and had to close her eyes, she writhed and made pathetic noises. When she became bored with telling the story over and over she stopped, looked at Jasper and said, "Mandrake Club — how do you do!"

*

"When I say piss up a rope, I mean it!" Jasper shouted at a waitress who asked whether he had a reservation. With that he entered and Mrs. Czap and Waldo followed. Clovis held Waldo's hand.

Jasper pointed to the ceiling, "There's your new home," he said.

Waldo looked up and saw a huge glass box suspended from the ceiling by cables. Inside the thing were a table and chair.

"Shall I get in now?" asked Waldo.

"Might as well," said Jasper.

"I'm going to miss you," Clovis said. "Hurry right down as soon as you finish."

The glass writer's-cage was let down slowly. When it reached the floor a waitress dashed over and snapped the door open. Waldo waved goodbye to his friends and got in. Then the cage was raised into the air where it swayed slightly. Waldo sat down at the typewriter and looked out at the club. He hadn't remembered that it was so pleasant. It was lovely with flowers and green ferns everywhere and filled with people having loads of fun. Heads turned toward Waldo and Waldo waved.

Clovis sat near the duck pond with Jasper. She flapped her hand at Waldo, then blew him a kiss. She loves me, thought Waldo. She's not kidding. Waldo was glad to be alive — all the people there in the club had come to watch him write. They cared. They loved him. And why shouldn't they? Waldo felt like weeping he was so happy. He had everything — looks, money, talent, the finest wig money could buy. He was free, no mom, no dad. God, am I happy! He looked at people going to and fro on the floor — everything was so gay. He flicked a switch on the side of the cage and everything went silent inside. He looked at the people, at Clovis. He was famous. He saw the people talking, their mouths moving. They were talking about him, saying his name and looking up at him. They knew he had them beat by a mile. He was famous. The king of the cage.

Down below on the dance floor a man came forward. The people who had been dancing went to their tables. Waldo flicked the switch again and heard the man introducing Mrs. Czap.

". . . really remarkable woman," the man said. "And it gives me a great deal of pleasure to present the amazing Mrs. Czap who has triumphed over sadness and is here to tell her true story. A whole host of famous personalities have written to say how deeply they too felt the loss, as if a child of theirs had passed on. Let me read just one of the many." He took a yellow piece of paper and began reading.

But the people would not listen.

"Czap-Czap-Czap!" they chanted.

"And that was sent in by none other than . . ."

"Czap-Czap-Czap!"

Waldo looked at them. They wanted to hear the details. They had had enough of introductions. They wanted flesh and blood. Even Clovis was banging her glass on the table and chanting the name of the bereaved woman. The master of ceremonies laughed and said, "I can see you're all as interested as I am to hear this terrific story. And so without further ado let me call upon Mrs. Czap. But before I . . ."

"Czap-Czap-Czap!"

". . . let her come up here I'd like to take a great deal of pleasure in announcing that today Mrs. Czap is fifty years young. Thankyouverymuch. And now" — a roll of drums — "Mrs. Czap!"

"There's something I want to get straight right off," said the voice from the stage. But Mrs. Czap was just seating herself and smiling at the audience. She did look a bit nerved up. The tape recorder continued in spite of her. She glanced around, heard her voice, then began moving her lips out of time with the words. It was like a foreign film that has been badly dubbed.

The people didn't mind at all. As she spoke they oohed and clucked.

Waldo turned up his microphone and tapped on the type-writer. *Fika-fika-fika-fika.*

The applause was deafening. The heads turned toward him and then back to the stage where Mrs. Czap ran on about the turtle, the bowl, the heartbreak of it all.

Waldo saw that the people were engrossed. He tapped again: *fika-fika-fika.* More applause.

It was like a tennis match. First the heads turned toward Mrs. Czap, listened to the story, then they heard the writer writing it down in his special cage and they twisted their heads up and listened to the tapping of the typewriter. They applauded both. They saw history in the making right before their eyes.

Waldo especially enjoyed it. Everything depended on his forefinger. He stared at his finger and then looked at the people. Then he made his finger trace an arc and go into a nose dive and land on a key. A stereophonic *fika* resounded through the Mandrake Club.

The people jerked in their seats and pounded the tables. They lifted their glasses to Waldo and then drank. And while this was going on *The Ballard of Willy Czap* played softly in the background.

Spotlights played on the writer's-cage. Waldo looked out — it was as if he was being held in a cloud. The glass was invisible and smoke drifted up from the crowd in hoops and wisps. Waldo felt like a bird gliding lazily through the lovely club and seeing everything and responding and being understood by his intermittent *fika-fika.*

". . . I was still getting sick every morning. But pretty

soon I stopped. Like before." Mrs. Czap stood, smiled and made a deep breast-jogging bow. Then, when the applause and whistles continued, she held her arms above her head and shook her fingers, as if she was drying her nail polish. Finally she blew kisses to everyone and sang snatches of *The Ballad*. She was a hit. The crowd went wild.

When she saw that the people wanted an encore she lifted her skirt and kicked her fat legs at the audience. And Waldo punctuated these kicks with raps on the typewriter.

Mrs. Czap stopped and blew more kisses, but Waldo could see her looking to the back of the dance floor where the ducks glided in the pond.

As a finale she went to the side of the pool and snatched a hapless duck by the neck and held him up to the audience. There were loud cheers as the duck was held aloft. He flapped. More cheers. He struggled to get free. A standing ovation. Mrs. Czap grinning and wringing the neck of the duck. Flowers tossed on the stage and a splatter of petals.

Once again Mrs. Czap bowed and, shaking her hips, waddled heavily off the stage. When she got to the stage door she blew another kiss to the audience and then flung the duck onto the dance floor as if she were throwing a bouquet of wet flowers.

A crowd of people ran onto the stage to capture the duck. They pushed and shoved and finally made a pulsing circle around the duck, each waiting for a chance to make off with a souvenir.

"He's coming to," one woman said.

"He is not!" said a man. "I can tell he's dead."

"He's alive!" said another woman in protest. "He's sleeping." The woman was indignant. She was wearing a paper hat that dangled foolishly from a hairpin and a long strand of hair. There was a mean frown on her face. A man next to her, holding her hand, took this as an opportunity to place his icy glass against her back. The woman bumped forward suggestively. Everyone laughed, then turned back to the duck.

"He's dead," a man said very simply.

Waldo saw Clovis pressing to the edge of the circle. In the center the golden duck lay on its side, its wings stretched out as if in flight. It seemed to Waldo to be rocking slowly, the white of its belly-feathers in contrast to the gold of its top-side. The feathers on its wrung neck prickled. Its beak started to open.

"Your ducks need oxygen," a man started to say seriously. He had a drink in one hand and a cigarette in the other. Confused, he tried to drink his cigarette. He spat tobacco and looked glumly at the frayed bulb he had produced on the butt.

Clovis's eyes were riveted on the duck and Waldo thought he saw the gold of the duck reflected in her eyes. She craned her neck to get a better look.

"Let's leave him alone," one man said.

"I want that thing," said another.

"If it's dead we gotta give it a decent burial," said the man with the tricky glass.

One brave man stepped forward and lifted the duck up gingerly by the neck. The people moved closer and closer until all that Waldo could see was the duck above the heads of the people.

"I got the bastard," the man said.

"He's breathing!"

"I can see his belly moving up and down!"

The duck seemed to be gasping, but it was hard for Waldo to tell. The feathers glistened in the half-light of the room and all eyes were turned upon the limp thing in the man's fist.

"We caught a duck!" a woman shrieked to the man next to her. The man nodded slowly and sipped his drink.

Then it happened. In one last desperate attempt to get away the duck flapped its wings and tried to take off. When the duck raised its wings a second time the man let go and the duck flopped with a futile *ploop* on the floor.

One woman screamed.

The circle widened and gave the duck room. But the duck just lay motionless, a lump of feathers.

Waldo saw Clovis whisper something to a man. He nodded quickly and then dashed out of the circle to a table where he grabbed a bottle. He charged back into the center of the circle, fell on his knees and struck down once.

At the very end of the amber swing the bottle and the golden duck met in an explosion, quick and muffled by the soft body. But the floor was hard and the bottle smashed — glass flew in all directions. The circle of people tightened again and huddled nearer the pile of glass and the feathery smithereens of the duck. The man got to his feet panting for breath. The neck of the bottle, still whole, was clutched in his hand. The duck had not even quacked. It gave Waldo the willies.

"Ya see him?" the man said to the crowd. "He almost took off!"

"Christ Jesus," another man said removing his steamed-up glasses.

Everyone puffed and shook his head, as if he had just run a race and was trying to get his breath.

"That was the biggest duck I've ever seen in my life!" one woman said leaving the circle.

Clovis smiled and offered the man some money. The man dropped the neck of the bottle and took the money. Clovis went back to her table and said nothing. The look on her face was beatific.

The circle of people stayed close to the duck, the mound of shards and blood.

*

So far, so good, Waldo thought on the way up to the hotel-room the next evening. The googly-eyed bellhop met Waldo and Clovis at the door and handed Waldo a small package. He grinned, then walked away.

"What's that?" asked Clovis inside the room. She pointed to the package.

"Present," said Waldo. "A surprise. Ha-ha."

"Is it?" Clovis spun all her clothes off quick as a wink. "Ha-ha."

"Ha-ha," said Waldo.

Waldo took off his clothes, turned out the light and joined Clovis in bed.

"The present! You forgot to give me the present."

"No, I didn't," said Waldo. "But before I give it to you you have to answer a few questions."

"The big reporter," said Clovis.

"Anyway," said Waldo, "first a few questions, then the present. That's fair."

"Give and take, that's my motto," said Clovis.

Waldo asked the questions. How many — to the nearest round figure — lovers had Clovis had? What was her earliest memory? If she had it to do all over again what would she be?

Clovis said that although she had had many lovers — too many to count in the time that remained before Waldo's evening show at the Mandrake — Waldo had been the best, the most rewarding. Her earliest memory was of her father hewing logs and saying that he had a piece of land, good land, rich land, and a hankering for putting seeds in that land and seeing things grow, things that he could love and cherish and sell. Clovis said she ran away when she was very young and sold her father's cow for a handful of bad beans, joined a circus, got herself raped by an oily little runt that juggled things. If she had it to do all over again, she'd take someone like Waldo and be satisfied.

"When I think about it," said Clovis, "I'm very happy. And usually when you think about these things you're not. But I am. I'm not lying either and, quite frankly, I lie all the time. In fact, I just lied to you about myself. Yes, I've known some interesting people, but my father, for instance, was a druggist. What difference does it make?"

Waldo tried to make his voice calm. "Well, it makes a difference if you're going to write a book about it."

"But I'm not, so it doesn't make any difference. I'm the only one that can tell if I'm telling the truth or lying. But I'd stake my life on the fact that someone in this world was a starlet, sold a cow, joined a circus, was raped by a juggler, fell in love with a young boy, told him so, and like that. And it might as well be me. I'm rich so I can talk like this . . . and no one is the wiser. It all makes a good story, don't you think?"

"Yes," said Waldo. "It does." He grinned at Clovis in the dark. She could not see him. He kept on grinning.

"Now the present?"

Waldo got out of bed and went to the table. He took off the paper and when he crawled into bed again Clovis said, "From now on I'm not going to lie any more. I'm going to tell you the truth. I'm a very foolish old lady and I was a very ordinary little girl. Please don't laugh when I tell you that I do love you — I'd do anything for you, anything. Sometimes I worry that you're going to run off with someone else. I've told you all those lies because you like lies. You're young enough so that when you're my age and you put all your lies together you'll see what the truth is. Now, after you show me that present I'm going to tell you the truth because I'm getting a little old for lying. But don't be disappointed if what I tell you is boring."

Clovis put her arm around Waldo's neck and gave him one of those kisses — the gluey-wet ones. Waldo fidgeted on the bed and took the present, a pistol, and quickly pressed the muzzle against Clovis, then deep into her — nearly up to the chamber of the pistol. He began firing.

Waldo was early for work at the Mandrake Club that evening. Jasper asked him where Clovis was and Waldo told him that she was in bed, which, after all, was the truth.

"Lots of people here tonight," said Jasper beaming; ever since Sybil Czap had been voted Mother of the Year and people had begun to send letters about *their* strange families Jasper had begun to look refreshed, younger, a bit bloodless yet prosperous. "They all heard about last night. Been coaching Mrs. Czap all afternoon on the duck bit. It's in the act now, see?"

Waldo barely listened. He had things on his mind. He got into his glass writer's-cage and set immediately to work. As he typed the first page of his story about Clovis Techy he was raised in the air, higher than the night before. But he did not notice it just as he did not notice the locked doors of the cage or the small size of the glass box which was now his home. He had already begun the story, dazzling, uproarious, hilarious, original, vivid.

He typed like crazy. He did not notice that Mrs. Czap had started her act and was being applauded. He did not notice that he was being applauded as he went *fika-fika-fika* through the story of Clovis, thinking only of her and thinking that it all mattered, even the lies, no matter how old you were. He could create and destroy and what he had just done in bed he would now do on paper; he had power over life and death, he was famous, he was rich, he had a nice simple glass writer's-cage. And he typed faster and faster (the people applauding the whole time) spilling the beans about Clovis as John, Morris, Fred Wolfpits and Mrs. Czap had spilled theirs. As his mother would someday tell all. You couldn't blame them for it. You couldn't blame him for it for that matter. You didn't have to love anyone for it though. It didn't have anything to do with love.